THE A~~MAZING RACIST~~

Half English, half Tibetan, Chhimi Tenduf-La grew up in Hong Kong, London, Delhi and Colombo, where he now lives with his wife, Samantha, and daughter, Tara. *The Amazing Racist* is his first novel. His second novel will be released later this year.

The Amazing Racist

Chhimi Tenduf-La

hachette
INDIA

First published in 2015 by Hachette India
(Registered name: Hachette Book Publishing India Pvt. Ltd)
An Hachette UK company
www.hachetteindia.com

SRD

ISBN 978-93-5009-912-4

Hachette Book Publishing India Pvt. Ltd
4th/5th Floors, Corporate Centre,
Sector 44, Gurgaon 122003, India

Typeset in Gentium 10.5/14
by InoSoft Systems, Noida

Printed and bound in India by
Manipal Technologies Limited, Manipal

For Samantha and Tara,
the perfect wife, the perfect daughter

Part I

one

Curry for breakfast was a bad idea.

I burped up cumin. Farted out the turmeric. My sweat was chilli powder and garlic, and the little pee spot on the inside of my khaki shorts had a hint of coconut milk in it.

'Chill,' Menaka said.

It wasn't so easy. The ceiling fan couldn't cool me, nor could the breeze as it slithered its way through the fingers of palm leaves.

Nine minutes to go.

A storm brewed in the distance and would be with us in moments. Menaka curled her highlighted hair around her neck, biting at the ends as we watched heavy clouds merge and separate, merge and separate. Four men in sarongs, the domestic help, lowered bamboo blinds wrapped in cellophane. A crow cawed, finding sanctuary under cover, a leftover bit of fish curry dangling from its mouth. The veranda lights faded off and then came back on again, brighter against the darkness of the rain which arrived in swirling sheets, like pages being turned in a book.

I pointed to the men. 'They knew exactly when the rain would come.'

'My father alerts them when he loses his satellite TV signal. They think he's a genius.'

So did I. From everything I had heard, so did I. Menaka's father, Thilak Rupasinghe – the great litigation lawyer and former

President's Counsel. A man so feared that it was said you had to look over your shoulder if you thought about him.

So what was I thinking?

Seven weeks after landing in Sri Lanka, six weeks and six days after having kissed Menaka for the first time, I sat outside his office armed with one question: Can I marry your daughter?

For a moment I was willing to overlook the sculpted lines of Menaka's figure, the milk tea colour of her skin, the glistening green of her eyes. The way she made me laugh. 'We can postpone, you know? Ask him in a month or so.'

Shaking her head, she leaned into me, her breasts squashing my instinctively tensed bicep. This was the first time I had seen her cleavage covered. The first time I had seen her without the purple lipstick she called Omega.

Seven minutes to go.

'Don't be silly.' She unwrapped a plaster and pressed it behind her ear to cover the tattoo of my name in Sinhala. I hoped to God her father didn't think she was hiding a hickey. 'There's a small chance he could like you.'

'A small chance?'

'Relax.' She closed her eyes and slid down the planter's chair. 'You're acting like you're about to meet the headmaster.'

Possibly the same fear, I thought, if my former headmaster had caught me in bed with his wife. And his mistress. And himself.

I slipped my feet to the end of my Bata rubber slippers. 'Do you think I have time to go change?'

'He's very punctual.'

'Sri Lankan punctual or English punctual?'

'He said five o'clock. That means five o'clock.'

Six minutes to go.

I began to pace up and down the veranda, past the row of antique chairs lined up as if in a doctor's waiting room. Outside, under the grape-sized raindrops, a fleet of classic cars rested, some on wheels, some balanced on rocks.

Five minutes to go.

A light went on in his office.

'Sit, boy,' a voice said in the tone of an earthquake. 'Beer, and my cigarettes.'

Even though her eyes were closed, Menaka must have sensed I was looking at her desperately. 'He's meeting my brother first,' she said.

Her brother's voice was meek compared to that of his father. I could barely hear him over the rain clapping against the roof tiles, so I squatted and pressed my ear against the door.

'You cut your hair yourself?' Thilak Rupasinghe asked his son.

'No, Thathi.'

'Then why the hell is it short here, long here, short here, bald here?' In between each word, the sound of a palm striking the skull.

No answer.

'Your head looks like a rambutan.'

Silence.

Four minutes to go.

'I read the letter you sent with your itinerary,' Mr Rupasinghe said, 'and I am happy for you to go on this trip, but *putha*, I have my rules.'

'Yes, Thathi.'

'Don't enter a girl's room. Don't speak to strangers. Don't drag your feet when you walk. Don't cross the railway line. Don't swim in the ocean. Or the pool. Don't drink. Don't smoke. You do drugs, I will circumcise you like a little Muslim boy. Don't wear dirty clothes. Don't wear short shorts. Don't buy those silly bangles you did last time you went to Unawatuna. Don't jump out of a boat. Don't jump into a boat. Don't go in anyone else's car if they have been drinking. Don't even look at a motorcycle. I worry about your life.'

'Thank you, Thathi.'

Three minutes to go.

'Don't look at white women's breasts. Don't eat from street stalls. Don't go to nightclubs. Don't have cake. Don't take your T-shirt off, because, *putha*, now you have breasts. Now come, come. Have a good time, *putha*.'

'Thank you, Thathi.'

'Wear sun cream. You're black enough already. Don't want people thinking my bloody boy is a labourer. Don't go in the sun unless you have to. Wear a hat. Put zinc on that huge bloody nose of yours. Don't use a squat toilet. Don't drink from a glass without rinsing it first. Okay, you bugger, have a good time.'

Two minutes to go.

'How old is your brother?' I asked Menaka.

The door opened. A man with short greying hair and a white beard hobbled out of the office. He wore clothes that were possibly too tight and trendy for someone in, I guessed, his mid-thirties.

'My name is Eddie.' I held my hand out to him.

He received it in a limp grip and laughed, pointing into the office. 'Good luck.'

'Where you going, Aiya?' Menaka asked.

'Stag weekend. I'm broke again, so had to ask the old man to pay.' He patted me on the back. 'The secret is not to listen. Just nod.' He kissed Menaka on the cheek, lit up a cigarette and ambled into the storm, not bothering to open his umbrella even when his smoke was extinguished.

Thirty seconds to go.

'Let's just forget it, baby,' I said.

Menaka grabbed my hand and yanked me towards the door, knocking before I could pull away. 'Don't drag your feet,' she said.

The office had legal books stacked on shelves right up to the fifteen foot ceiling. Either side of a mahogany desk, sculpted onto a lion's legs, stood rusted metal statues of warriors brandishing spears. I almost didn't notice Thilak Rupasinghe sitting between them. Under a ceiling fan that turned the room from light to dark on the whim of its blades, the comb-over on his balding head barely cleared the desk. Leaning on his elbows, which were at shoulder height, he didn't lift his gaze from the newspaper in front of him, which he read through silver-framed glasses perched above his jet-engine nostrils.

I felt my eyes widen, almost theatrically, when I saw the hole in his neck close up. It wasn't an open hole, of course, but the trapezius muscle on his right shoulder was missing.

'To what do I owe the pleasure of my daughter visiting me twice in the same week?' he began.

'I want you to meet someone,' Menaka said.

His gaze lifted and locked on me for a split-second. His eyes were Tabasco-red, the lids above them hanging like bats from a tree. He beckoned Menaka over with a curl of his fingers. She bent down in front of him and he kissed the top of her head.

'And who is it you want me to meet?' He looked at me again for an even shorter time than before.

'My boyfriend.'

'Another one? Ah, very well, Nangi, very well.' He stared past me towards the door and sucked on his cigarette.

Menaka fake-coughed and shoved a finger against my chest.

Mr Rupasinghe pulled his office chair on its wheels around to the side of his desk and shuffled his bum forward so that his feet were flat on the ground. I inclined towards him at the same time as he stood and we almost banged our heads – or at least his head nearly hit my chest. Leaning back, I tried to shake his hand but he bowed to me.

'I am Thilak Rupasinghe,' he said. I smiled, I think. I tried to, at least.

'And you are?' he asked.

'Edward Trusted.'

'Pleasure to meet you.' He turned to face Menaka. 'Now, darling, where's this boyfriend of yours?'

I chuckled, assuming I was meant to, turning it into a cough when I realised I was not.

'Is there something wrong with your friend?' Mr Rupasinghe asked.

Menaka rested the end of her fingertips on my shoulder. 'This is my boyfriend.'

Mr Rupasinghe laughed as if he had been told the funniest joke of all time – pausing for breath, slapping his own legs, reaching out for a high five. Just before I had to decide whether to join in or not, he stopped and slammed his palm against his desk. 'Don't even joke about such things,' he growled.

'I'm not joking,' Menaka said.

'You must be,' he said.

I turned to the door. 'I better go and leave you to –'

'You're going nowhere, chalky,' Mr Rupasinghe tugged me back by my belt. 'Sit down.' His voice echoed off the walls of books, across the veranda, out through the classic cars and back again. I sat down before the echoing stopped.

'This is a sick prank, Nangi, one I wouldn't play even on your absconding mother.'

'You told me to settle down,' she said. 'That you wanted grandchildren soon.'

'Not with blonde hair and blue eyes. Or worse still, can't have bloody grandkids looking like Burghers. This won't happen.'

'It just might, Thathi.'

As it darkened outside, the effect of the fan's blades on the light became more prominent. It was not quite as intense as flash photography, but the inconsistency of the light made me dizzy and I didn't think I'd be able to stand up even if I had been given permission to do so.

Father and daughter stared at each other. Inches apart. Daughter taller than father, fairer, more muscular. But father unquestionably more intimidating.

Three minutes of silence.

They slumped on either side of the desk, so I moved myself up against a wall a bit closer to the door.

Mr Rupasinghe leaned forward and said, 'Nangi, he's white.'

Menaka looked at me. 'See, I told you he'd notice.'

'What will people think?'

'That he uses Fair and Lovely.'

I made a whoops face when Mr Rupasinghe looked at me. Not a wise move, but I didn't really know what else to do. He literally bared his teeth at me, so I pointed to the door and mouthed, 'Shall I go?'

He blocked the exit and looked at Menaka. 'If you're ready to settle down, there are many proposals for you.'

'I'm not that desperate.'

'There is a lawyer who lives in Sydney. Has a 3D television and a sari-wearing mother.'

Menaka ambled towards me and sat on my lap. Was she trying to get me killed?

'A doctor from LA, with two SUVs and an exceptional horoscope. An engineer who studied at Cambridge and has perfect vision. All Kandyans. Fair-skinned.' He pointed at me. 'I mean, not like chalk-fair, but fair.'

'Eddie's a teacher.'

'And you think a teacher can support your lifestyle?'

'He doesn't always intend to be a teacher.'

'Does he always intend to be white?'

'I tan easily,' I said.

Menaka and her father looked at me, as if I was a gatecrasher at their private party.

'Please get off his lap or I can't speak to you properly,' Mr Rupasinghe said.

I shoved Menaka back onto her feet before she had a chance to defy her father again.

'Edward.' Mr Rupasinghe pulled his office chair next to me. 'I have nothing against you or the colour of your skin. But you are clearly white, which suggests to me that both your parents are white.'

I nodded meekly.

'That's surely how it should be. It just keeps bloodlines strong. Do you agree?'

'Yes, in some respects, but –'

'Thathi, he's just scared of you, that's why he's agreeing.'

'No, the boy is talking sense. Did my daughter bully you into this relationship?'

Lifting her hands up in prayer, Menaka said, 'Please, Thathi.'

'You see, she has a history of picking men I would not approve of just to annoy me. There's been a Tamil, a Muslim, a Burgher, a clerk, a baker –'

'You're ridiculous,' she said.

'– a candle-stick maker. None of them have lasted three months. She doesn't even introduce me to the ones she's dated for less than eight weeks.'

'We met seven weeks ago,' I said, immediately regretting it.

'Well then, you must be *so* special.' His smile was crooked, either because he was faking it or because surgery had left him like that. 'I give you another month.'

'This is different,' Menaka said.

'And how so?'

'Eddie, ask him.'

I spat it out. Like jumping into an icy swimming pool off a ten metre board. No thought. Just took the plunge.

'Can I marry your daughter?'

The ambulance taking Thilak Rupasinghe to Durdan's Hospital broke down on the way but got there eventually. The doctor said Mr Rupasinghe was weak, still, from his cancer and had suffered a stress disorder, which was only partly due to me. It turned out that Mr Rupasinghe had been indicted on charges of political interference. The crime: representing the family of a big shot MP who had been murdered by a bigger shot MP.

The doctor suggested that he take a break from work. Menaka insisted.

'He got cancer five years ago,' she told me. 'Doctors gave him six months to live. But he beat it, while still drinking, smoking and playing golf.'

This made me feel a little more manly and less embarrassed about the potential soiling of my pants in his presence. After all, he scared the shit out of cancer too.

'They had to cut the growth off his neck. In all, he had twelve operations and a great deal of chemotherapy. So, you know, it would mean a lot to me if you two got along.'

I had work the next day, thank God, so I didn't need to decide, then, whether or not to visit a man I needed to like me. Two double periods of A-level Economics. I strayed from my lesson plans and set a timed essay for each of my classes. When I felt my phone vibrate in my pocket, I knew it was Menaka.

'Maybe we've rushed into this,' I typed. 'Maybe there's no hurry. Neither of us will be thirty for a few years. Thirty's a good age, no?'

'Indika, don't look at Nabil's essay,' I said aloud, not seeing whether Indika had actually looked at Nabil's essay, but it would have been in keeping with character. He apologised.

'I won't let him rule my life,' Menaka messaged back. 'He's a cantankerous old bastard. He can't shower me with his misery.'

I put my phone off during the meeting about the school play I had been pencilled in to direct. Nothing like being thrown in at the deep end in my first few weeks. Perhaps my fault for saying, on my CV, that I had directed three plays when I was at university. I don't think I had even watched three plays. I wanted to do *One Flew over the Cuckoo's Nest*, but I had to hear out the other members of the PTA. The Head of History suggested we stage the Ramayana, the English teacher proposed *Romeo and Juliet*, the music teacher wanted us to do *Grease*. A Japanese parent, an old lady in a kimono, painted nails, netted hair, said, 'What about we do Pussy in Boots?'

Oh sweet Jesus. I raised a cardboard file to the level of my face, but I could hear a snigger across the room. I held my breath, tears forming in my eyes, my shoulders bouncing.

Pussy in Boots!

Sweet sweet Jesus.

Four deep breaths, I lowered my file and bit the inside of my cheeks.

'I'm sorry,' said the Principal, 'what play was that?'

Oh dear god, no.

'The Pussy in Boots,' Mrs Akimoto said again.

Up went the file. Up and down went the shoulders.

I agreed to do *Grease* because that was the only word I could get out without my laughter erupting across the room.

I breathed again when I got into the corridor, once the giggling exhausted itself. But it started again when I imagined the name, Pussy in Boots, in neon lights above a strip club, until –

Vibrate. A message from Menaka. 'My father wants you to come to his hospital room.'

I sneaked into Durdan's Hospital, allowing myself to get lost, hoping Mr Rupasinghe would change his mind. But no. As soon as I poked a fraction of my head round his door, he pointed to a chair inches from his bed.

'I've got some time off,' he said, 'so since my daughter is rather stubborn, I have promised to get to know you. I sleep at midnight and wake at six. Otherwise I can pretty much be with you all the time.'

I brushed down my hair. 'I don't think that's necessary, but thanks.'

'You don't want my company? But I thought you desired to be my son-in-law.'

I faked a smile. 'I'd love your company.'

'Great.' He reached a hand out to me. 'I'll be your shadow, your stubble, the T-shirt that's too tight to get off, the band-aid stuck to the hair on your knee. I'll show you Sri Lanka, the Sri Lankan way. Hope you like spicy food.'

two

I had arrived in Sri Lanka seven weeks earlier to take up a teaching position at an international school on a two-year contract. I remember exiting the airport with no idea what was ahead of me, no idea if I could actually teach, no idea if I would make friends, and no idea if I would be considered attractive to South Asian girls. What I did know was that it was unrealistically humid. I knew this because my white shirt became transparent with sweat, introducing my nipples and the hair around them to the Sri Lankan public immediately.

I had to navigate my way through baggage trolleys laden with double-door fridges and TVs and then dodge the eighty-four people waiting at the arrival lounge per one arriving relative. Everyone smiled, their white teeth like paparazzi camera flashes engulfing me. I was told I would be 'found by the school driver', so while I waited, I amused myself by picking faults in the signage around the exterior walls of the airport.

My favourite: 'If you see a suspicious package, *warm* others.'

I watched commandos in ill-fitting shades cradling machine guns as if they were babies. Between them a chubby guy with a Hitler moustache called out Eddie, my name, to anyone white who passed him, male or female.

The school driver.

I got into his van and asked him lots of questions, but a

cacophony of bus horns and the whines and barks of stray dogs drowned out his answers.

The roads looked like they had been thrown on top of each other, the odd train track too – a rich kid's messy playroom – as if the cars had been hurled away in a tantrum, pointing in any direction, in any condition. The street signs hung at weird angles, some tilted by tropical winds, some faded by the sun. Behind them, the green and yellow of the most beautiful landscape imaginable.

We bounced along past super-centre shops and mud-huts, McDonald's and one-legged beggars, Buddhist monks and heavily armed commandos. The driver only stopped at zebra crossings if the pedestrians bothered to hold up their hands to signal that he should. If they failed to do so, it appeared that they were fair game to oncoming traffic.

'Put the AC up, please,' I said at least fifteen times.

The driver wobbled his head, grinning. The AC remained on low, so I opened my windows and a lop-sided bus screeched past, spraying me with powdery exhaust fumes.

The over-riding smell was of bonfire smoke. But as the clouds gathered and the streets became dark in an instant, the rain doused out the smoke and steam rose off the asphalt. Street vendors covered their ware in plastic sheets and motorcyclists gathered under the patched-up roof of a military checkpoint.

'I've never experienced rain like this,' I said. 'I can't see anything past the windscreen.'

'Don't worry.' The driver had a high-pitched giggle. 'Neither can I.' He put his headlights on full beam and used his horn a little more.

The rain went as quickly as it came, and the road ahead of us looked like it had not seen any of it.

We got stuck in a traffic jam, caused by an untethered cow

straying into the middle of a junction and exacerbated by the driver trying to manoeuvre the school van onto the pavement on the other side of the road.

'My boss is want you to touch him,' he said in a squeaky voice. 'You would like to touch him?'

Um.

'Here.' He offered me his mobile phone. 'You can touch him from my phone.'

Ah, get in touch.

'The phone is ringing,' he said.

'Hi, Eddie, this is Jimmy Walsh. Short notice, mate, but how'd you fancy a cricket match today?'

'I'm a bit rusty, but –'

'Watching, mate. Watching. The third ODI at Premadasa.'

Jimmy Walsh was at my new rented accommodation before we got there. He looked oriental from the front, but from the side, he was clearly Caucasian – the Keanu Reeves of expatriate school owners. He was unshaven, in knee-length shorts and a muscle T-shirt which gave as much prominence to his pot as to his biceps. He slid open the van door and grabbed both my hands. 'Eddie Trusted, the man, the legend. Good to be here?'

'Great to be here,' I said.

He handed me an envelope. 'Your school ID card. Carry it whenever you can for security checkpoints with a copy of your passport and visa. Immigration insists we remind new teachers that this visa is only valid for paid work at the school. Nothing else.'

He pointed at the driver. 'Mendis will take your bags inside. It's a nice little place. The landlord's drunk ninety-five per cent of his waking hours, but if you drink with him for the remaining five per cent, he may not charge you rent.'

'So I'll have a quick shower and we'll head off?' I asked.

'No time.' He handed me a can of beer and pointed to a tuk tuk. 'Get in, mate.'

We must have had time after all, because we stopped for a couple of arracks at the Cricket Cafe, next to a sign that pointed out the direction and distance to the most iconic cricket grounds in the world. Jimmy told me arrack, a coconut-based spirit, was an acquired taste. I envisaged a protracted acquisition period.

By the time we joined Jimmy's friends at the ground, the rain burst out of low clouds, but not for long enough to flood the pitch. We drank Three Coins lager, smoked Gold Leaf, danced *baila*. I'd never danced *baila* before, but not knowing the steps didn't distinguish me from any of the other experienced proponents of the dance.

How to dance *baila*? Drink as much as you can and stumble around with your arms in the air, mumbling in beat.

'This music is hilarious,' I said. Trumpets, drums, strangled cats being played by comatose men in matching clothes. 'Bloody awful.'

Jimmy wrenched me in a headlock, tugged at my hair and turned me to face him. 'Don't say another word. It's a national institution.'

'This band?' I asked.

'*Papare* bands, they're called,' Jimmy said. 'Music of the people.'

'They're actually playing music?'

'Quiet, dude.' Jimmy pointed at the big screens around the ground. These *papare* bands were everywhere. 'Just dance. It makes sense when you dance.'

I danced – hopping from one leg to another, arms in the air, bouncing against sweaty bodies, with my eyes closed.

When I opened my eyes again, the silhouette of a girl just a few feet in front of me blocked out the floodlights. She mimicked all my dance moves – also, I assumed, the glazed look on my face. She had a girlfriend either side of her, giggling, egging her on.

I dropped my arms to my side, so did she.

I shook out my hands, so did she.

I bounced on my right leg, so did she.

I bent to touch my toes.

So did she.

I lifted my shirt.

She froze.

'You got played,' one of her friends remarked. The girl turned to say something back, so I took the opportunity to look her up and down.

She wore micro-shorts. Her legs were strong; thicker ankles than most Sri Lankan men there at the match, let alone women. Her arse was a bicycle rack, a credit card slot. Her skin, the softness of air-brushed advertisements, the colour of caramel ice cream.

She faced me again. 'Menaka,' she said. Her emerald eyes reflected the floodlights and the rain. 'Your dancing is, you know, interesting.'

'Your moves were amazing,' I said.

'I learnt from the best.'

Her friends still flanked her. Saying nothing. Smiling.

'Sorry, you said your name was?'

'Menaka,' she said. 'Like Tenaka with an M.'

'Tenaka?'

'You are?' she asked.

'Eddie.'

'Like Teddie, with an E?'

'Precisely,' I said.

She pointed at Jimmy Walsh, sloping out of the ground with his friends, likely too drunk to remember that he employed me, let alone brought me to the cricket match. 'You need a lift?'

'I think I do, but I don't know where I live.' I got on my toes to see if I could see Jimmy and Co.

Menaka copied me, on her toes, hand above her eyes. 'You've got his number, I assume.'

We left the ground in an unregistered Range Rover, some guy driving in shades even though it was night and only one in four street lights worked. From time to time he lifted his sunglasses to have a peek at Menaka's legs, but when he tried to touch them, she slapped his hands away. 'Get over yourself,' she said. 'I was drunk.'

The smiley girls were in another car somewhere so the conversation in the jeep was limited. Menaka spent all her time on the phone making plans for us, so I tried to ask the guy driving some questions which he tried not to answer.

I knew right away that Menaka was about as different as anyone I had been attracted to before. As an only child, I needed to get my way, so my girlfriends tended to be the type not to argue their own case. The kind of girls who were, I guess, a little insecure.

But Menaka – I had never met anyone so confident before, and even though this turned me on in some ways, it also intimidated me. Underlying it all was the fact that she was, quite simply, the best-looking South Asian girl I had ever seen in my life, and for some reason, I was going through a phase where white just didn't work for me.

After Menaka's non-stop calls on two phones, we ended up sipping champagne in the shallow end of an apartment block swimming pool, overlooking Galle Face Green, an army camp and Colombo port. I swam in my boxers, Menaka in shorts and a see-through white T-shirt, under which she bulged out of a black and white pin-striped bra.

She handed me something that looked like an out of shape cricket ball with green sprouting out of the top.

'Mangosteen,' she said.

'What?' I asked, wary of moving too far away from the wall and into the glare of the underwater lights.

'It's a fruit. Dig your nails in to open it.'

I did as instructed, peeling off the dark purple skin to expose a white segmented fruit.

'It looks like a woman's parts, doesn't it?'

'I'm not sure I see the resemblance.'

She slapped her hands against her mouth. 'Oh my God, you're married.'

'What?' I lifted my hands above the water. 'No.'

'Then how do you know what a woman's parts look like?'

'Well, I have, you know...um...I'm –'

She put a finger to my lips. 'You're not saying...' She closed her eyes. 'God forbid, you're not saying that you haven't saved yourself.'

'For marriage?' I asked.

'For marriage,' she said.

I couldn't speak. Like in one of the accountancy exams I left England to get away from, I had no thoughts in my head other than wondering what Macaulay Culkin was doing now.

She looked at me, her head bowed, lips curled down.

'You're shitting with me, aren't you?' I asked, a smile spreading across my face.

'Indeed I am, *machang*,' She took it upon herself to splash me. 'Well, are you just going to look at it all day?'

'The fruit?'

'No, my you know... Yes, the fruit.'

'Am I supposed to bite into it?' I asked.

'No, you're meant to smother it on your skin.'

I laughed and took a bite of something that tasted like strawberry. Or was it kiwi? Or plums? Mangosteen was all of these and none of them. Delicate, exquisite, melt-in-your-mouth, sweet but sour – tropical bliss!

'Is that your new favourite fruit?' she asked.

'It is,' I said.

'Favourite cake?'

'Battenberg.'

'Same here.' She clapped. 'Your turn.'

'Weights or cardio?' I asked.

'Weights.'

'Same here. Biggest worry if you were a man?' I asked.

'Not being able to handle the flu. Biggest worry if you were a woman?'

'The fact that I have a penis,' I said.

She laughed. 'Favourite food?'

'Biryani.'

'Unexpected.' She closed her eyes and nodded. 'Nice. Favourite singer?'

'Prince,' I said.

'You like if I was your girlfriend?'

This was all faster than expected so I played it cool. Sure, I couldn't believe my luck but there was a thin line between keen and desperate. 'I guess we could give it a go.'

'What do you mean?' she asked.

'Okay, I'd love it if you were my girlfriend.'

'Awkward.' She laughed. 'I was asking you if you liked the Prince song, "If I was Your Girlfriend".'

Awkward indeed. I placed an imaginary shotgun in my mouth and acted out blowing my own head off, collapsing under water. That would impress her, I thought for a second, until I remembered she wasn't a fourteen-year-old aspiring accountant. When I came up for air, she was leaning away from me, looking over the city. 'I wouldn't rule it out though,' she said to the clouds. 'You fit in with my type.'

'And that is?'

'White,' she said.

I smirked. 'You're my type too.'

'Brown?' she asked.

'Beautiful.'

Her turn to act out sticking a shotgun in her mouth. 'That could have cost you, but I feel good. Let's play make believe. Say we hang out, we get on, we kiss...'

She moved her head towards mine, but as soon as I did the same, she backed away. 'We date, we get serious. How will your parents react if you say you have a brown girlfriend?'

'I doubt they'll even notice.' I flicked water off my hands and reached for a cigarette from the edge of the pool. 'And yours?'

'Mum wouldn't care because she left us when I was a kid.'

'Your dad?'

She chuckled. 'My father wants me to end up with someone of the same race, religion, caste, literacy, social club, library, the same town, the same street, the same house. Someone with the right horoscope, the right job, salary, house, car.'

'And skin tone?' I asked.

'And skin tone.'

'So being white may not work in my favour?'

'He'd likely disown me.'

'Maybe when I meet him, I won't tell him I'm white.'

'He might notice.'

We shared a laugh and then drags of the cigarette. We'd only met a few hours earlier, and I had no idea if this relationship would go anywhere. In past relationships, the parents had liked me more than the actual girl herself. So being told that her father may not accept me made me feel tense, and that was before I knew anything about him. At the same time, I liked that we were talking about this, because it meant she could have feelings for me and I was certainly falling for her.

'What will he do if he doesn't approve?' I asked.

'Best case, cut me off financially. Worst case, he'll hunt you down and turn you into a eunuch. '

'He'd never catch me. I'd leave civilisation, grow a moustache and hide in some unpronounceable province of northern Sri Lanka, wearing a sarong and guiding a bullock across a paddy field. You'd come?'

'Let me think about it,' Menaka said. 'No, I think I'd prefer you as a eunuch.'

three

It took Menaka seven weeks to present me to her father as the new man in her life. It took him a further seven weeks to think about allowing me anywhere near his extended family. When the day came, I wished it hadn't.

Mr Rupasinghe's cousin Gehan and his wife Thilini were throwing a party; everyone invited seemed to have been told it was in their honour. Yet Menaka warned me I would possibly be the only guest not related to, sleeping with or doing business with the hosts.

Mr Rupasinghe sent Sidath to pick me up. Sidath wore a badge that read 'Trainee Driver'; he drove with learner plates and insisted I sit in the front with him since I had a licence. He handed me a sarong and vest, along with a note in the fierce hand of Mr Rupasinghe. 'Dress traditional,' it read.

I arrived at the dinner in sarong and vest. Everyone else wore jeans and shirts, skirts and blouses. They laughed at how I had used a belt to keep my sarong up. How high up I wore it. 'Like a skirt,' Thilini said in a mock Tudor accent.

I wanted to say surely a sarong is a bloody skirt. I wanted to tell Thilini she looked ridiculous, that her face-lift made her look like she was about to scream. I wanted to point out that her house was like a junkyard sale. But I didn't.

Gehan and Thilini had managed to fill one of the largest sitting rooms I had ever seen with four different sofa sets: one red leather, one cream fabric, one wood and twine, and one rattan. They had gold-framed posters on the walls – a tourist poster for Sydney, a poster of a leopard and two of white babies. The look was completed by a porcelain dog, a dolphin lampshade and a statue of a fairy. I would have guessed they were poor relatives had I not seen their fleet of luxury cars outside: a Jaguar, a Range Rover and a Hummer.

Mr Rupasinghe nudged me onto the veranda with the men. I had the chance to wave back into the living room at Menaka, but that was about it. The men knocked back wholesale large shots of whisky and expected me to keep up, so when Thilini put out the food I rose and grabbed a plate.

'Do you have a penis?' a man asked. He looked to be my age, and had a very muscular upper body, but matchstick legs. The zig-zag effect on the side of his beard was probably intended to be cool, but if you ask me, a man who goes to that much effort on his looks is not cool. He was clearly artistic though, because his hair was set in a layered sculpture above his threaded eyebrows.

'What was that?' I asked.

He took my plate away from me. 'Only women eat now. We booze.'

'Oh.'

'My name's Gayan.' He looked back into the sitting room, at Menaka, toe-to-arse, arse back to toe, then toe to arse to head. 'So you're with my second cousin?'

I wobbled my head.

Gayan watched Menaka turn, his gaze locked on her breasts.

'You're her second cousin?' I asked.

'And best friend.'

I shuffled towards Mr Rupasinghe on the veranda when he summoned me with a clap and an odd kissing-like noise. I saw Gayan chatting with Menaka among the junk of the sitting room, giggling, tugging her arm, stroking her bloody hair. I wasn't proud of this, but when I had checked Menaka's mobile the previous night, there were thirty-two messages from Gayan in one day. Thank God they were related.

Aiya winked at me and pointed to a back entrance. 'Let's get out of here,' he said. 'Hit the casino?'

Boy, was that tempting but how could I have left Menaka? More to the point, how could I have left Mr Rupasinghe without destroying all chances of him liking me?

I explained myself to Aiya with a pretend slit of my own throat, just before Mr Rupasinghe introduced me to people who made me sign up for car clubs even though I didn't own a car. Mighty Mini Club, Italian Car Club, Mercedes Club. Land Rover. Bajaj.

'Eddie's an economist and a qualified accountant,' Mr Rupasinghe said to the men. 'All of you can send him your cash flows to check.'

'Damn good,' Gehan said. 'I'll give you a shout tomorrow.'

'Keen golfer too,' Mr Rupasinghe said.

'Just a beginner,' I said.

'Modest as always.'

We sat down for dinner at a plastic table in the kitchen.

'You want fork and knife?' Gayan asked me.

'Bloody crazy,' Mr Rupasinghe said. 'Bugger eats with his hands.'

What about the food? Yes, they had made a special 'mild' chicken curry for the white man. It seemed they had run out of chicken and subbed it with more red chilli. Even my nipples began to weep. I tried to wipe the tears out of my eyes with my fingers but they had curry on them, so it made things worse.

'Eat, eat, you bugger,' Mr Rupasinghe said. 'You want Aunty Thilini to think you hate her cooking?'

'I love it,' I said, and ate some more. The walls of my stomach caught fire and I had dragon breath. I tried to stand, almost toppling the plastic table wedged between two piles of stacked chairs. Mr Rupasinghe directed me to a tap to wash my hands. Bonding, I thought, when he nudged me upstairs where Gehan's fellow gem merchants had convened a meeting on the terrace to take a stand against discrimination. Mr Rupasinghe, in front of everyone, offered me money to replace the melted ice in their glasses and to light mosquito coils.

'Good to have a white man serve us for a change!'

The indignity. I accepted.

The four men sat in a circle around a potted tree that dropped *araliya* flowers at their leathery feet. Around them, coconut shells dipped in kerosene burnt light and mystery into proceedings. Each of the men, Gehan included, wore cologne so strong that the aroma battled with that of the dried fish, chilli and onions being fried downstairs. The sparkle of fireflies got lost in the collection of thick gold chains, watches and bracelets on display.

Gehan was the alpha male of the gem merchants. His rice belly was the biggest, his gold chains the darkest and thickest and his voice the deepest. The other men, apart from Mr Rupasinghe, all looked like Gehan. They had tiny legs and huge bellies, wore their trousers up to just above their knees, and had done up only two buttons of their crisp linen shirts. Each of them, like Mr Rupasinghe, used the thinning hair on the sides of their heads to comb over their bald patches.

Gehan stuck his fist into the bowl of cashews I offered him. Rubbing his rice belly, he said, 'These bloody white countries have to keep their business to themselves.'

Mr Rupasinghe coughed and pointed at me. 'Tell him.'

Bandula Balasuriya, a gem merchant from Ratnapura, scrunched up his nose and looked me up and down. 'Your people, I tell you.'

Gehan held up a hand. 'Not the bugger's fault. It's these bloody Norwegians. Mouthpieces for the Tigers.'

Bandula spat chewed cashews at the terracotta-tiled floor. 'Bloody baskets.'

Sipping on his whisky, Mr Rupasinghe looked up to the full moon in an ackowledgement that it should have been a day of abstinence. He clapped his hands and glanced in my direction. 'Black Label.'

This was my cue to go downstairs to pour Red Label into a Black Label bottle. I passed Thilini and the other gem merchants' wives who were not allowed entry onto the roof terrace because the discussion about discrimination was deemed to be above them. The wives openly flaunted their newfound wealth, each of them too fair in skin tone to have married the men upstairs without some financial gain.

'Has anyone seen Menaka?' I asked.

A lady, whose flab flooded out of her sari, raised a foot to show off the Jimmy Choos stretched across her soles like plasters. 'She left with Gayan. Dancing.' The other ladies dipped their fingers into metal bowls of hot water and lime to wash off the fragrance of curry and the yellow of turmeric.

I messaged Menaka asking why she had left without me; because there was no reply, I tried to call her. She didn't answer by the time Mr Rupasinghe shouted for me. I returned upstairs; as soon as I came out onto the terrace, everyone stopped speaking.

'They have a question for you,' Mr Rupasinghe said.

'It's a simple question,' Gehan said.

Bandula cupped himself. 'Tell me, boy, what do you think of the driving in this country?'

A mosquito bit at my bare ankle. I bent to slap it away

and when I raised my head again, I was face to face with Mr Rupasinghe.

'Answer the question, *suddha*,' he said.

'It's interesting,' I said.

The gem merchants laughed enough to fall almost off their chairs.

But not Mr Rupasinghe. He looked deadly serious. 'Define interesting,' he said.

'Well, let's just say the drivers aren't sticklers for rules.'

'So you think we lack discipline?' Mr Rupasinghe asked.

'You could say that.'

'Interesting.' Gehan chuckled.

'What about our roads?' Bandula asked. 'Bloody mess, no?'

'Well yes.' I smiled. 'They're a little behind the rest of the world.'

'In what way?' Mr Rupasinghe asked.

Even though I had drunk enough to make an elephant impotent, I knew I had to choose my words carefully. 'I'd say there's something quaint. Like an English village, but here in the city.'

'Quaint,' Bandula tried to say. 'Like an English village. How so?'

'Cows crossing the road. Some roads too narrow for two cars to pass each other without one pulling over.'

'Ah yes,' Marlon Ratnayake, the drunkest of the lot, said. 'Bloody pain those roads.'

'There are no such roads,' Mr Rupasinghe said.

'Yes,' Marlon said. 'No such roads.'

'What else?' Mr Rupasinghe asked.

'Potholes,' I said. 'A lot of potholes and constant road works.'

'The bus drivers?' Gehan asked.

'Psychopaths,' I said. 'How come they never get busted?'

'Most private buses are owned by retired cops,' Bandula said.

'That's just a bullshit rumour,' Mr Rupasinghe said.

'Yes,' Bandula said. 'A rumour. Bullshit.'

Marlon leaned forward with an empty glass. 'Top me up please, *putha*.'

I obliged him. 'My biggest observation is about the pedestrians.' I spread my arms. 'However big the pavement is, they walk on the road.'

'Why do you think that is?' Gehan asked.

'I don't know, maybe it's as simple as no one telling them.'

'See,' Mr Rupasinghe said to the others. 'Whatever they say, however nice they pretend to be to us, it's impossible to ignore that these white people think we're imbeciles.'

I said, 'I never even –'

'You implied,' Mr Rupasinghe said. 'In your tone. Like we're sweet little mindless idiots.'

'Not you guys, I mean –'

'The poor?' Mr Rupasinghe asked. 'But they are our people. Sri Lankans.'

'Go easy on the boy,' Gehan said. 'Let's just put a shot. Fill up the glasses, *putha*.'

'We drink from glasses,' Mr Rupasinghe said. 'Not out of our hands as you probably imagined.'

'Sir, please, I –'

'Have you heard of Anuradhapura?' Mr Rupasinghe asked me.

It sounded familiar. 'Is he a cricketer?'

Everyone laughed so much they spat out much of the whisky from their mouths.

Except Mr Rupasinghe. 'Part of our cultural triangle. The ruins of an ancient and advanced civilisation.'

'Boring place,' Bandula said. He looked at Mr Rupasinghe. 'But also fascinating.'

Mr Rupasinghe pulled out his phone. 'Aiya, tell Menaka we, as a family, are taking this boyfriend of hers to Anuradhapura tomorrow.' He hung up the phone and faced me. 'When you see how magnificent our history is, you'll realise you're just a philistine.'

'Ah.' Marlon leaned forward. 'One of my Arab buyers, he is also from Philistine.'

In Anuradhapura, the sun was directly above us. I could feel the skin on my exposed neck tighten as if the moisture was being sucked out of it. It felt crisp to the touch of my fingers, with cracks suggesting my skin would peel that night. My right flip-flop slipped off in front of me, displaying bikini lines on my foot; the gap between my toes, and the lines of the straps remained white. The rest of my foot was crimson. Now I understood why Mr Rupasinghe, Menaka and Aiya carried umbrellas even though there wasn't a cloud in the sky. Now I understood why they were using them under the glare of the sun.

I plundered my way through four litres of water, each bottle costing me more the further into the site we went, and I still felt hungover and dehydrated from the night before.

Amongst the ruins, we were watched by hundreds of monkeys. Touts approached me to sell whatever they had, but each time they inched too close, Aiya pointed at his father, said something in Sinhala, and they turned away.

'You see this civilisation?' Mr Rupasinghe swivelled round

on his walking stick, pointing out the various ancient ruins of Anuradhapura.

'Which one is that, sir?' I asked.

'I hope you're not being smart,' he said.

I wasn't. There was a great deal to take in and I was trying to match each structure to what I had read in a guidebook on the six-hour journey up here – the bell-shaped dagobas up to a thousand feet tall, the raised platforms of the monastic buildings, and, my favourite, the *pokunas*, or the bathing tanks.

'No, sir,' I said. 'It's all quite mind-boggling.'

He pointed to a *pokuna*. 'Freshwater in there back in the day. Irrigation.' He pumped his chest out, lifted his chin. 'The first century after your Christ, we built reservoirs and irrigation systems still in use. What were you white buggers doing back then?'

'I doubt he was born, Thathi,' Aiya said.

'You were hanging from trees and shitting out of windows,' Mr Rupasinghe said.

'He's still doing the latter.' Menaka said.

Mr Rupasinghe pointed his open umbrella towards a dagoba. 'And you guys look down on us?'

Aiya said, 'Thathi, to be fair –'

'You'd do anything to be fair,' Mr Rupasinghe said.

Aiya closed his eyes and lifted his eyebrows. 'To be fair, it doesn't look so great on us that we were such an advanced civilisation then and now –'

'Because these white buggers raped us.' Mr Rupasinghe pointed at me, his finger shaking. 'Stole our cinnamon, plundered all our resources. The harbour of Trincomalee. These peasants. These bloody peasants. Well?' He turned to me. He wanted a response.

'Sorry?'

'That's it? Apologies? I'm taking legal action against the United Kingdom. Why should we suffer in poverty?'

'We're hardly poor, Thathi,' Menaka said.

'But our people are.' He rotated on his heel, pointing. 'Look at all of this. We're being restricted from returning to our former glory.'

Menaka said. 'It's the war.'

'And who started that? The bloody Brits, bringing more Tamils here, giving them more prominence than they deserved...'

He stopped and clutched his chest, slumping back on a rock.

'We can't blame the Brits,' Menaka said.

'Exactly,' said Aiya. 'It doesn't help us if we deflect blame.'

'You've been doing that all your life,' Mr Rupasinghe said. 'Nothing's your fault. You can't find a wife, it's because woman are scared of me, right? Can't get a job? I made you too dark.'

'We shouldn't have tried to recreate past glories after independence,' Menaka said. 'Sinhalese glories. Isolated the Tamils.'

'If they didn't like it,' Mr Rupasinghe said, 'they could have gone back to India.'

Aiya said, 'You can't talk like that.'

'You don't like my accent? Want me to speak more white? More Tamil?'

'Thathi, seriously,' Menaka said. 'Who's your best friend?'

'Subramanian.' Mr Rupasinghe turned to me. 'He's Tamil, which I think is my daughter's point.'

'My point is, you're scaring Eddie into thinking you're some kind of amazing racist.'

'I am just a man of passion.' He slapped the back of his right hand into the palm of his left. 'Not like this lethargic boyfriend of yours. Not like this lazy bloody brother of yours.'

'You're so perfect,' Aiya said.

Mr Rupasinghe said, 'I'm super perfect. Compared to you, I'm the king coconut of perfection. The dagoba of perfect.'

Each of his words echoed around the ruins like the voice of a ghost ruler from the past. Menaka stood by his side and draped an arm over his shoulder.

'Thathi –'

'Yes, I know, keep cool, keep calm.'

'I'm sure Eddie gets the point,' Aiya said. He pulled me under the shade of a tree's branches and summoned over a man carrying two baskets strapped across his shoulders. 'Aloe Vera?'

I lit a cigarette. 'Will you and your father be cool?'

'He'll ignore me for the rest of today,' Aiya said. 'Then tomorrow he'll wake me up early and chat as if nothing's happened.'

'He forgets?' I asked.

'Not always, just when it suits him.'

four

I scampered into the froth of a dying wave, blinking at the setting sun's reflection off the turquoise sea. Fishermen in catamarans fought to bring their catch under control as grey clouds encroached on the red-tinged sky above them. The monsoon breeze, whistling through the coconut trees, dropped a vendor's frangipani flower within my reach. I stooped to pick it up, while watching a sunburnt woman clamber up an elephant's raised leg. The mahout, tucking a bundle of cash into his sarong, flashed the tourist a toothless smile and poked at the elephant with what looked like a devil's trident.

With my gaze shifting between the elephant and the turds it had just released like cluster bombs, I stepped forward into a hole in the sand, which crumbled under my weight. A crab scurried out of its burrow, up the beach towards where the girl of my dreams wrung water from her silk hair. She wore a green bikini top, a lighter shade of her eyes, which looked like small sails stretched across giant masts. As she lifted her blue and orange beach wrap, it fanned out in the wind like a peacock's tail. Bending forward, the line of muscle on her thighs rippled, a clear separation from her hamstrings; not too much muscle, just enough. Her bikini bottoms showed more bum than I thought suitable amongst people who didn't try to hide that they were staring, but I stared too. Her abs, almost a six pack, maybe a four pack, but again just right.

Calculated, devised, the perfect body.

I stood next to her, the frangipani extended in front of me, but everything I had planned to say was lost like the crab without its home.

Because this was Menaka.

Against the backdrop of palm trees and cloudless blue skies, she looked spectacular, like a monument of a god I had begun to wonder if I should believe in. Should worship.

I couldn't say it. I couldn't confront her about ignoring my messages for the last two days. As much as I hated waiting by my phone for a response that rarely came, this made up for it. The sight of her. The way she moved her limbs, stroked her hair. The way she winked at me when I approached her. The power she had in her beauty. In her confidence in that beauty. Her smile. The white teeth, the eyes almost closing, causing temporary wrinkles. The smile that said, I love you, I need you. The smile I couldn't see when she wasn't answering my calls.

She leaned forward and kissed me, tasting the salt in my mouth, her arms hooked up under mine, her palms flat against my tensed traps. Holding my hands, she dropped back onto her rattan beach mat and pulled me down next to her. She stroked the ends of the hairs on my chest. Brushed the sand off my stomach. Let her damp hair tickle my neck.

'You wanted to talk about something,' she said.

'It's nothing, really.'

'Then why the text saying it's really important?' That bloody smile again.

'So you do read my texts?' I asked.

'Of course I do.'

'But you don't reply?'

She utilised her four-pack to lift herself onto her elbows. 'I do, mostly, no?'

'Sometimes I get a word or two.' I sat up and tried to light a cigarette with a local match, challenging at the best of times, but near impossible in the sea breeze.

Menaka watched me burn out my fourth match. 'I'm not as fast with my fingers as you are.'

'What?'

'With texting,' she said. 'It's not my thing.'

'But you don't answer my calls either.' I buried my sixth used match into the sand.

'I'm one of the few people in this country who still thinks it's rude to use a mobile phone in someone else's company.'

'I wouldn't mind the odd message to say you're okay. I worry.'

'You shouldn't.' She grabbed the box of matches off me and lit the cigarette at the first attempt. 'I have my sound off most of the time.'

'Lots of meetings, these days?'

'Tons, but I like it, baba.' She kissed me around the face so softly, it could almost be imagined. 'It's what I've always wanted to do.'

'But you think about me?' I asked. Ugh. Pathetic.

'Of course.' She rubbed her hand up my thigh, over my shorts. 'But, baba, I know you. If I was one of those girls who texted you every time I thought about you, you'd swim a mile away.'

I had joined Menaka down south on one of the few work gigs she encouraged me to come to. Working with Habitat for Humanity and Odel, Menaka was project-managing a scheme to build houses for those who had lost theirs in the 2004 tsunami. Once our work was done, I jumped on a train back to Colombo, my legs dangling out the open doors, enjoying the breeze and the view of the sun setting below the ocean. Menaka travelled further south to help Gayan with one of his do-gooder projects. I gave up on calling Menaka after the first few hours and, instead, had a good feed with Kenneth McApline, the half Scottish business guru who always had an alcoholic way of making me not worry about something.

But the more I drank, the more I had an urge to text her. It had been about fourteen hours since I had heard anything from her, but I knew she was okay because she had posted, on Facebook, a picture of herself and Gayan with some orphans.

Then I sent her a message which, sober, would have made me cringe, as much as I would have done, again if sober, after playing air guitar with Kenneth on the dance floor of Silk nightclub. The message said: 'Do you really love me? If so, how much?'

She didn't reply. But she posted another picture, on Facebook, of Gayan carrying a child with no legs onto the beach.

The longer she ignored me the more I obsessed.

Then I got this message:

'I love you so so so so so so so so so so so so so so so so so much. You make me the happiest. You make me smile. Never leave me, okay? Tomorrow at 11.30 meeting with Taru about the wedding at Gallery Cafe.'

It made me feel like I did when I first called the hot girl from my neighbouring boarding school and she agreed to come to our midnight barbecue. Like I was in love for the first time. And after Kenneth got bored of me gushing about Menaka, I celebrated the night away at a casino with Aiya. I went to bed with a smile on my face even though I had lost twenty-five thousand rupees of my money and a further fifteen of Aiya's. On top of that, I still owed Jimmy Walsh the three months' advance that I had taken to buy Menaka's engagement ring. The one she chose.

I passed out pretty easily.

The next morning the landlord, a can of beer in his hand, woke me at six-fifteen. 'Thilak Rupasinghe called. Get dressed.'

'What?'

'He's got something fun he wants to take you to.'

'Oh how kind,' I said. My head had a cricket match running inside it, *papare* bands, *baila* and all. My skin itched. My throat was sandpaper. I was still pissed.

'Classic Car Club meeting,' Mr Rupasinghe said from his convertible MG.

'But I promised Menaka I would take her to the wedding planners.'

'You told the gem merchants you would love to see all the classic cars. Now, you ungrateful little shit, I wasn't planning to go myself. I'm here for your bloody benefit.'

'Thank you, sir, but Menaka?'

'I'll tell her, don't worry. She won't mind.'

There was no way Menaka would take that well. 'I'll call her from the car.'

'No, no, you're driving.'

'But I'm probably over the limit.'

'No such thing here,' he said.

No sooner had I got in the driver's seat, a crow shat on my head. Mr Rupasinghe's crooked smile was limited to the side of his face closest to me. All the classic cars in front of us passed through a green light, but I slammed down on the breaks when it turned red.

'We'll lose them,' Mr Rupasinghe said. 'Go, go.'

'It's red, sir.'

'Don't be such a pussy. Just drive, drive, drive.'

I did as told because it would have been stupid to defy him. As I nudged out into the junction, a bus coming at full pelt through his own green light swerved out of our way, the passengers hanging out the side of the bus swung off their feet.

A cop in khaki with white sleeves and white gloves blew a whistle.

'Stop,' Thilak said.

'Licence?' the cop asked.

I gave him my UK one.

'You don't have international licence?'

I shook my head. I think he assumed I meant yes, so I said, 'No.'

'Big problem,' the cop said. 'Very big. Have you been take the alcohol?'

Mr Rupasinghe looked at me and nodded, the bastard!

'Last night,' I said.

'You is still have the smell. Very big problem. What we can do?'

Mr Rupasinghe was out of the MG and in another classic car before I had time to shit myself.

His licensed driver, Ranjith, turned up out of nowhere and took the MG key from me. I climbed onto the back of the cop bike without a helmet. The cop grabbed my hands and wrapped them around his love handles. 'Hold on tighter,' he said. 'Tighter, tighter.'

I couldn't say his body odour was altogether pleasant. Interesting, not pleasant, but I stopped noticing when I saw all the classic car pricks laughing at me. The cop waved at them, soaking in the applause, as if he was a streaker at a cricket match returning to the stand of the drunkest people.

'Bad luck,' Mr Rupasinghe shouted out. 'Hey, *putha*,' he said to the cop. 'Shouldn't he be wearing a helmet?'

When we stopped at the station the cop gave me a ticket for riding on his bike without a helmet.

Two hours later, I was still at the police station. Dusty files boxed me in like a child's fort. No threats, no reassurances, no good cop, bad cop. Nothing.

My phone buzzed. Yes, I know, I should have used it before.

Menaka: 'Where the hell are you? We're meeting Taru now.'

Shit. 'I'm at the police station. Went through a red light.'

'Really? Ugh! Pay them.'

'What???'

'Pay them about two thousand and they'll let you go.'

'A bribe?'

'They call it a spot fine. Just pay. Taru's super busy, I told you that.'

'I only have one thousand five in my wallet.'

'Oh bloody hell. Charm them. Give them one-five, tell them they speak good English. Which station?'

'Not a bloody clue.'

'Call Thathi and ask him to speak to the cops. They're terrified of him.'

'He was there when they busted me.'

'Figures. Okay, ask the cops what station and I'll send Aiya with some money to pick you up.'

Aiya arrived in nineteen minutes. I was out in twenty-five, but we got stuck in school traffic.

'You're screwed,' Aiya said, a smirk on his face. 'Menaka's wedding has to be exactly one hundred per cent like clockwork.'

'I know, but what to do?'

'Reconsider marrying her.' He chuckled as if sharing an inside joke with himself.

'Nice try, bro, but I love her too much for that.'

He pretended to vomit, jerking forward in the driver's seat. 'Well, beware, the rest of your life will be like this. Running after Menaka. Doing everything Menaka says.'

I drummed my palms on my thigh. 'Don't worry your pretty little head about that, big guy. I'm the last person to ever get pussy –'

'It's nothing to be embarrassed about. I was halfway through a double Thai massage at Angsana and somehow, twenty minutes later, I ended up at the police station to pick you up. Just because she called.' He smiled. 'But I'm family. I'm trapped. You still have a chance to get away.'

By the time I arrived at Gallery Cafe, Taru had left and Menaka was sitting with Annika, one of the owner's two beautiful mixed-race daughters. I slipped into the chair that must have just been vacated by Taru. 'I need something sweet,' I said. 'Too much curry these days. No spice, just something sweet.'

Annika ordered me the Jaggery Creme Brule. I had a spoonful and my tongue clapped. It was served with *thala gulli*, a sesame-seed sweet. Amazing, and with a nice cold Lion Lager, and a small wash in the gents, I began to feel a little human again.

'Baba,' Menaka said. 'Now don't kill me, but Annika and I have got a meeting with the Defence Ministry about getting provisions up north so I'm going to have to pull out of the Yala trip.'

Music to my ears. I wasn't keen on another trip with Mr Rupasinghe after the Anuradhapura debacle. 'Not a worry at all. I'll happily spend the weekend by the pool.'

'But Thathi has booked everything.'

'Can't he cancel?' I asked.

'He never cancels.'

'Aiya's coming, I hope.'

Menaka stroked the inside of my forearm and it tickled. 'He's got a date with some hot sari-wearing woman.'

'Annika, what about you?'

'Do you not listen?' she asked. 'Meeting. Defence Ministry.'

'So, are you saying, just your father and me?'

Menaka nodded, a mischievous smile developing across her face.

'Surely not.' It was genuinely humorous to think how absurd the situation was. 'You're sending me on a road trip alone with your father? This is almost –'

'It's hilarious,' Annika said, getting up to greet the friends she was actually there to meet.

Menaka held my hands across the table. 'I think there's a slim chance you may make it back alive.'

꙳

It was just Mr Rupasinghe and me in a one-bedroom bungalow in Yala National Park. At least we had two separate beds.

Mr Rupasinghe wore a spider-web print sarong and a curry-stained white vest that looked like a bra above his rice belly.

We drank arrack on the veranda and Mr Rupasinghe dragged his way through a packet of Gold Leaf without offering me one.

'You know, people sleep out here sometimes. Gayan did so last month and woke up with a cobra under his chair. You like snakes?'

'Hate them,' I said.

'They're harmless as long as you don't attack them. You wouldn't do that, would you?'

'Of course not.'

'Then you've nothing to fear.' Mr Rupasinghe struggled out of his planter's chair and flicked his remaining arrack out of the glass onto the red clay garden. 'Just try not to roll over on one in your sleep. They may assume that to be an attack.'

'Snakes can come into the room?'

'No, and neither can leopards, bears or wild elephants.' He entered the bedroom, chucked out a striped sheet and locked the door behind him.

Oh.

I felt torn between wanting to sleep and wanting to stay awake so that I didn't roll over onto a snake. I would have texted Menaka to bitch about her father, but I had no signal. Mosquitoes bit at my ankles because the sheet was too short to cover my whole body. I repositioned it and they bit my chest. Worse, they buzzed around my bloody ears so I tugged the sheet over my head. Then they mauled my knees, my shins, in between my toes.

I couldn't see if there were any snakes, so I lowered the sheet again, my legs balanced on the extended arms of the planter's chair. The oil lamp burnt out and all I had left was the stench of kerosene and the light of the half moon.

And noises. Slithering sounds, footsteps, trumpeting of elephants. Rumbles. Growls.

Two hours in, the bedroom door opened. 'You're still alive?' Thilak Rupasinghe asked.

I said nothing.

'Well, I thought I heard a bear. Careful of those buggers. Vicious.'

I'd had enough. 'Please can I come in there?'

'Do you still want to marry my daughter?'

'Yes.'

'Prove it.' He locked the door behind him once more.

I slept a bit and had dreams as follows: jumping out of the reach of a bear's claws; hiding in a tree as an elephant charged it; nookie with Menaka; a snake between my legs.

Mr Rupasinghe had enough time before I woke up to make me a cup of tea, which I drank with a hand above my eyes, blocking out the sun.

'I had a deal with my daughter,' he said. 'And to be honest, I'm scared of her. She's too irrational, too rash. Capable of anything, so I daren't betray her.'

He pointed to a rock near the veranda, behind which a cobra fanned its head in the face of a mongoose.

'I promised her I would give you a chance. Give you a test. And I did. I tested you. Threw all that I had at you and you've stood there and taken it like a pussy-whipped little white boy. But you know what?'

I assumed I had to reply. 'What?'

'You've impressed me. I'm never going to pretend, even vaguely, that I have a scintilla of joy that my baby girl is marrying a *suddha*. But, maybe I can...'

Silence. I wanted him to say it.

'Maybe I can give you my blessing.'

'Oh my god!' I lunged into a hug position, which had to be one of the more idiotic things I had ever done. He somehow looked down at me even though I was a good foot taller than him, raising his palm, pushing me away.

'I can't tell you how happy this makes me,' I said.

'Back down, puppy,' he said. 'Stop licking my face.'

'I wasn't, was –'

'You put one bloody foot wrong, you bugger, and I will have you deported before you can say go easy on the chilli. And even if you don't put a foot wrong, you never, and I repeat never, treat me like you'd treat your parents. Here, you respect your elders. You don't question us, don't speak unless you're spoken to. You don't voice your opinion, advise me, you don't even tell me I look good unless I ask you. Understood?'

I wobbled my head.

'Menaka's a flight risk, like her mother. She doesn't like commitment. She doesn't like to feel tied down. Do you acknowledge that?'

'Well I –'

'Do you acknowledge that? Yes or no.'

'Yes, sir.'

'Then call me Uncle Thilak.'

five

I peered out of the French doors; the blue of my room's private swimming pool merged with that of the sea below.

Two days without Thilak. Bliss.

Saman Villas in Bentota, a room on a cliff.

Bliss. Bliss. Bliss.

Uncle Thilak told Menaka to get her own room because we weren't married yet, so she was in one directly above me.

'He'll never find out if I stay in yours,' she said.

'I promised him,' I said.

'What a pussy.'

I was sure Uncle Thilak would have paid a waiter to spy on us. Maybe the pool boy. Maybe Uncle Thilak was disguised as the pool boy. Wouldn't have put anything past him.

Menaka went for a massage so I perched at the end of the infinity pool, my arms dangling over the cliff face. To the right, swaying palm trees lined the golden beach; grown men threw frisbees, young boys played with toy guns and white women tested the laws of how much skin they could show. To the left, through gaps in the bamboo fence, I could see into the private pool of the suite next door. A man, tanned, chiselled and smug, untied the strap of his girlfriend's bikini top, but then saw me.

I turned away and reached for a beer and a cigarette, closed my eyes, took stock of just how fantastic things were. Yet, as usual, I overdid the sun thing. I think I could have fried fish on the end of my nose. So I skidded my way across the wooden floor of my room, to the open rain shower, and everything, even my sunburn, seemed irrelevant. Hearing the sound of the waves when applying after-sun lotion, served as a reminder of just how lucky I was. Lucky to be away from Uncle Thilak's noise.

I unpacked my stuff, washed and jogged upstairs to Menaka's room. Knock knock. Gayan answered.

What?

Gayan?

The shower was on in the background.

'Is this a coincidence?' I asked.

'Uncle Thilak wants me to be your best man, so I'm here to get to know you.'

'I can't choose my own best man?'

'Do you even know Uncle Thilak?' He laughed. A creepy preacher kind of laugh.

I slouched on the edge of the bed. 'Fine then. Let's get to know each other.'

'We can do that tonight,' he said. 'I'm sharing your room.'

'I see.' So that's how Uncle Thilak planned to keep track of me.

Gayan sat down on the sofa, his legs on the coffee table, his fingers on the remote control. Behind him, Menaka waltzed out of the bathroom, her hair in a towel, the rest of her naked.

'Menaka!'

She jumped back, held a hand to her bare chest. 'Oh God, you scared me.' She strutted around the room, her breasts bouncing, the little fat on her arse wobbling. 'Gayan's staying tonight.'

'Yes, I know.' I gestured for her to cover up.

'He's my cousin. Not like he hasn't seen it all before.'

Gayan pointed the remote at the TV as the channels flicked through Cartoon Network, Baby TV, some Tamil music show, Chinese news, then six blank channels. He only found something that could conceivably be of interest to him after Menaka slipped into a bathrobe.

I followed Menaka through the saloon doors into the dressing room. 'You don't think that's weird?'

'What? Gayan being here?'

'Well yes, and –'

'That's pretty standard Thathi practice. If I admit to going on a trip with a man, Gayan chaperones me.'

I pointed my finger back into the room. 'I mean you parading about naked in front of him.'

She laughed and slapped my back. 'You're so silly. He's like a brother to me.'

'That makes it perfectly acceptable.'

'You English are so stuck up sometimes. Just chill, okay. It's only my body.'

'Did you see the way he was looking at you?' I asked, spit coming out of my mouth.

'We're not even married yet and you're getting paranoid. Please, okay, I can't handle that.'

We drank cocktails on the wooden deck above the infinity pool. Sea water splashed against the cliff beyond the pool, then up over us, temporarily dousing the burning coconut shells that provided our light. It would have been romantic were it not for Gayan sitting between Menaka and me, one hand on each of our legs. I still couldn't make him out. Was he here to cock things up for me, or was it that Menaka was his only friend? Either way, it annoyed me, but there was something noble in Menaka not turning her back on him. Noble, but irritating.

I was always in direct competition with Gayan, whether Menaka realised it or not. I can't remember a time when she let his calls go unanswered, regardless of whether we had been in bed or in a cinema or swimming pool, for example. I'd caught Gayan threading Menaka's eyebrows; caught her waxing the hair below his eyes. It was Gayan who always knew where she was; Gayan who went to Zumba classes with her; Gayan who she talked charity work with, who she slagged off her friends to.

Menaka's phone rang to the theme tune from the *Exorcist*. 'It's for you.'

I accepted the phone from her, covering the mic. 'Who is it?'

'Thathi.'

'What? No way, please say I'm on the loo.'

Gayan held his fingers to his ears. 'Answer the damn phone, please.'

'You're on the loo, are you?' Uncle Thilak asked. 'Number one or number two?'

'Bit of both.'

'Now, *suddha*, if you're going to marry my little girl you need more than a teacher's salary, would you agree?'

'I guess.'

'I checked. You finish school at four-thirty if you have play practice, three-twenty if you don't.'

Creepy that he knew that. 'Yes, that's right.'

'My legal practice is getting a little out of hand. Staff too big. Too many lawyers and trainees. I need this managed. I need taxes monitored, billing receipts. We can't balance the books. I need budgets and cash flows and bottom lines. I need reports. Now, *suddha*, you were an auditor, no?'

'Well I did two years at E and Y but then switched to teaching.'

'Oh,' Uncle Thilak said. 'You didn't qualify?'

He knew that. I didn't need to answer.

'No matter,' he said. 'One thing you white guys have is systems and checks. You're all anal, all pedantic. But that's good in this case. What's your salary at school?'

'One hundred and ten thousand rupees,' I said.

'Basically a thousand dollars a week?'

'A month.'

Pause.

'Oh dear. That'll barely pay for Menaka's pedicures. Let me think. Maybe if you work three hours for me a day. We're open pretty much all night, so let's make that four hours extra every day, takes you to about eight or nine. Maybe we double your salary. Sounds good?'

I had bugger-all choice and I knew it. 'Sounds great, thank you.'

The phone went dead at just the moment that I noticed Gayan and Menaka sucking straws out of the same glass.

I didn't see much of Menaka alone over the next couple of weeks, but I settled into the teaching and moonlight accounting and my wallet started to swell a little, but only because I had no time to spend any money.

Menaka and I had separate accounts, a good thing since she was out every night at some dinner or another. Sure those meals were free, but the new outfits she wore to each of them weren't. Often her outfits cost more than the amount raised at the fundraising event for which the outfit had been bought.

I almost pointed that out one day, but then thought to myself, Gayan wouldn't do that.

⁓❦

'My staff thinks you're a very good accountant,' Uncle Thilak said. 'For a *suddha*.'

He'd signed me up for a Typist of Sri Lanka fundraiser and the Coconut Plucker's Association Sports Day, but I got used to this. I was flattered, in some ways, that he wanted me to come with him even though it was obvious I was just filling in for Menaka and Aiya who had the strength and position to say no occasionally. With all the buffets I had developed a rice belly and a numb tongue. My tolerance for arrack grew by the day and I had mastered the art of addressing people I didn't recognise by calling them *machang*. Menaka got busier and busier with whatever cause she involved herself in. I think she talked such a big game that she began to find she had to back it up to save face.

And, of course, she cared.

After four nights of not seeing her, I messaged her to rant, but instead of replying she just turned up at her father's practice.

Uncle Thilak remained on his medical ban from working, so his office was empty. Menaka lifted a foot against my bum to push me through the oak door, which she then locked after her and further secured by shoving a chair against it.

'Let's go to the staff loos,' I said.

She shook her head and unbuttoned my shirt, kissing down my chest, my chest hairs rising against her lips.

My belt buckle. My zip. My trousers.

'This is too dangerous,' I said. But too magnificent. Too amazing. Too oh yeah, oh yeah. 'I want to see your body.'

Her dress over her head. Her bra catapulted and her panties

kicked towards the door. Her fingers against my back, then her nails, not tickling, just expertly arousing my skin. Her breath on my neck, her hands through my hair.

Her whispers. 'I need you.'

'I need you too,' I said.

'Be quiet.'

She kicked me in the stomach, onto Uncle Thilak's leather chair. His throne. The chair in the portrait behind his desk.

Now, my bare arse against it. Sticking to it. Sweating on it.

Leaning over me, she swooshed her hair across my bare legs, against my chest. Her muscular legs held her above me without touching. Teasing. The greatest bloody tease of all time.

I reached out a hand to touch her but she slapped it away.

'Don't be a pervert,' she said.

'I need you,' I said.

'Don't be desperate.'

Her legs on either side of me, she lowered herself. The hairs on our skin met, danced, bonded.

I tried to pull her down.

'Behave,' she said.

A click at the door. My eyes opened.

The door handle turned. The chair against it moved.

'Shit,' she said.

'Shit, shit, shit,' I said.

Trousers up, gadget caught in zip. I wanted to scream. Couldn't free it. Almost tripped over the chair. Shirt on, buttoned wrong. Not the time to worry about that.

Shit. Shit.

'Open the bloody door,' Uncle Thilak's voice boomed.

Menaka fought to get into her skintight dress. 'It's open.' She waved me away. 'Get under the desk.'

Light from the reception crept through the opening in the door. Getting bigger. Getting bigger. Once all of me was under the desk, my foot jammed.

'Nangi, what the hell is going on?' Uncle Thilak asked.

'I came to see you.'

'That's odd,' he said. 'I'm hardly ever here.'

'I know, but I needed to find you. To thank you for accepting Eddie.'

Uncle Thilak grunted, his feet shuffled. 'Where is he?'

Sweet Jesus. Menaka's panties still on the chair by the door.

'I sent him out to get us some *kothu*.'

'Nangi, he's paid to do my accounts.'

'I know, I know, but I wanted to see you alone.'

Little feet in shiny shoes very close to the desk. 'Well, what is it?'

'When we have the wedding –'

'If we have the wedding.' He pulled out his chair from behind the desk. The portrait light above it reflected off the grooves of my arse print.

Menaka said, 'Thathi.'

His eyes diverted away from the chair just in time. He sat, his feet almost touching mine.

'I'm going to miss having a mother there.' Menaka cried. Oscar stuff. The fluctuating rhythm of her breath. The sniffing.

The shiny little shoes moved away from me. 'I often regret marrying such a selfish woman, but if I hadn't, I wouldn't have you. At the wedding, I'll be your father. And your mother.'

'So you'll sanction it?'

'Let's go meet Taru,' he said.

The door closed behind them.

Menaka is amazing, I thought. The way she could manipulate Uncle Thilak. The way she could manipulate anyone.

There was something intriguing about that. Something powerful.

Something sexy.

Certainly sexier that the sweaty arse print I had to slap off Uncle Thilak's chair.

six

If I hadn't uncovered the discrepancy in his books, I wouldn't have had the confidence to approach Uncle Thilak's office again.

I knocked and entered before he said, 'Come.'

Dropping a thick receipt book on his desk, I announced, 'One issue is your guys don't do monthly bank reconciliations.'

'That's not illegal.'

'No, but it's the easiest and surest way to chase money. It's a record of cash. Very basic. Have to do it monthly.'

'So you've tracked down the funds?' Uncle Thilak asked.

'Well, yes and no.'

'No time for amateur dramatics here, *suddha*. Answer my question with just a yes or a no, not both of them.'

I squatted by the arse-print chair, lowering myself until I was the same height as him. I put a file on his lap, which made him give me a dirty look.

'Too many cash payments. Hard to keep track of, but we have invoices here for things that have never been delivered.'

'You mean?'

'Fraud. Let me give you an example. Forty-two new chairs at twenty-one thousand rupees each for the boardroom. But those chairs that we have there, I've checked, they are at best worth nine thousand each.'

'Sons of bitches. Is that it?'

'Lots of examples of this.'

Uncle Thilak rose to his feet. 'Who?'

'Don't have any proof but I have my –'

'Give me a bloody name, you bugger.'

'Navin Perera.'

Uncle Thilak spoke into the intercom. 'Get me Gunesekera in the garage in the next twenty minutes. And get Navin Perera in there in thirty.'

'*Suddha*, you have done well.' He put a hand on my shoulder for a quarter of a second, before wiping his palm against his trouser leg. 'Very well. I want you to stay and enjoy this with me.'

'What's that, sir?'

'The law doesn't always work. I want my people to know something like this can never happen again. I have a man who works for me. Does my investigations on criminal cases. Collects money owed to me too. Anil Gunesekera, AKA Leg-breaker Gunesekera. He's going to have a little word with Navin Perera and then I want Navin Perera to walk through the rest of the office, his nose in a pulp, his lips split, his eyes closed. Blood dripping onto his stupid tight shirt and pointed shoes. Not on his trousers. Must make the bugger walk without trousers.'

What the hell had I done? A man skimmed some money and falsified invoices, and now he was about to be beaten in front of me. Paraded through the office. In front of me. As if I had endorsed his beating.

'Uncle Thilak, I think we better be sure before we do anything. I have no proof it's –'

'Don't talk bloody cock, you bugger,' he said. 'You English never make mistakes. You have systems.'

'But in this instance I think I may be wrong.'

Uncle Thilak laughed. 'Face or stomach?'

'Sir?'

'Are you going to go for his face or his stomach?'

'But, surely...'

Uncle Thilak draped his arm over my shoulder, his fingers tickling my upper pecs. 'Now, it is your choice to join this family. I'm not forcing you. Far from it. But in accepting you, I'm of the understanding that you approve of me. Is that not the case?'

'I respect you, but...'

Pushing me through the oak door frame, he said to the receptionist, 'Make the garage out of bounds for the next hour and a half.'

An hour and a half of beating, I thought, the lift door closing behind us.

'There are no buts. You want to be part of this family, you do things our way. This is our way. Face or stomach.'

'Stomach.' I pictured the smile Navin Perera always wore below his thick moustache. Pictured it dripping blood.

All the garage lights were off but for one that flickered directly into our eyes. The footsteps were of wooden-soled shoes, but I couldn't make out the person wearing them.

'Gunesekera,' Uncle Thilak said.

It's too late, I thought. I couldn't even run. I was trapped in the basement garage, about to beat the shit out of a guy who had two small kids. One kid had a learning difficulty. No schools would take him. I gave his father advice. Now I was expected to give him a thrashing.

'Leg-breaker Gunesekera,' I said, just as he came out of the shadow.

A man slightly taller than Thilak. A man who wore his trousers up to his nipples and carried a briefcase like a baby. A man with loose curls drooping over his wide-framed glasses.

'Hi,' he said in a helium voice. 'He's calling me Leg-breaker now, is he? Used to call me Orgasm-faker Gunesekera before.'

His handshake was limp.

'Gunesekera,' Thilak said, 'does my hiring and firing for me. The labour courts here provide a lesson in frustration. It doesn't matter if someone has a case or not, they can screw you over, at least in terms of time and comfort, by taking action against you. Even a petty thief like Navin Perera.'

I gave Uncle Thilak a so-we're-not-going-to-kick-his-head-in-look. He responded with a I-was-pulling-your-bloody-leg-you-jackass-look. Leg-breaker Gunesekera gave me a what-are-all-these-strange-looks-you're-giving-each-other-look.

'I'll deal with this,' Gunesekera said. 'Recover what we can, get him to sign things saying he won't go to court if we don't go to the cops.'

'And everyone can live happily ever after,' Uncle Thilak said.

꒰꒦꒱

I had a good economics class on the Monday back at school. Told jokes, some kids laughed, some didn't. Some got high marks. Some didn't.

I received an email saying Jimmy Walsh wanted to see me. I marched to his barely used office, sat at his round table, not at all scared. He was my friend more than my boss.

'Mate, mate, mate,' he said. 'Maybe I didn't make this clear enough.' He dropped a file in front of me. 'That's a copy of your visa. Read it, will you?'

I started reading and knew where this was going. The gist of it was that I could only work for the school and no one else. Guess I shouldn't have told the Head of Mathematics, Mr Samarasekera – Hard Sum as he was known – that I was moonlighting outside school. He was pissed off that I earned more than him because of the colour of my skin. Dude had been at school six years, me less than six months.

'Look, it's not a huge crime and I'm sure there's some misunderstanding,' Jimmy said. 'Immigration has been in touch with us. So I have to ask, have you done any paid work elsewhere?'

'No,' I said, my mouth all but closed.

'Well...' Jimmy stood up, opened the door for me. 'I'll take your word for it. But if they prove otherwise, we could be in the shits. Write me a letter, say you've done no paid work anywhere but here. Sign it. Then at least the school's off the hook.'

'I'll get on that straight away,' I said, farting fear.

'But don't put anything in writing unless you're sure about it.' Jimmy rolled a chair to me.

I sat.

'Are you sure, Eddie?' Jimmy asked. 'Are you damn sure they've got nothing on you? They assure me they have. Anything? Even one rupee exchanged hands for any work done?'

I rubbed my upper lip. My skin cracked against my finger; I bit the inside of my cheeks; squeezed my nuts together between my legs. Simple techniques in self-harming. Thinking. Thinking. Thinking.

'Well, I get money from Menaka's father to do his accounts.'

'Ah, Jesus, Eddie why didn't you say? A one-off?'

'Kind of.'

'You go into his office, have a contract, a desk, a company email address?'

Yes, no, yes, no, I nodded. 'What does this mean?'

'It means I should let you go and advise you to get out of Sri Lanka tomorrow before your visa is cancelled. Jesus, Eddie, you've put us in a very bad position here.'

'I should've known. Sorry, Jimmy. Give me a chance and it won't happen again.'

'It's not us, mate. We haven't got a damn say in this. You've broken the conditions of the visas we've signed up to.'

'Wait, so –'

'You're here illegally.'

'You're pulling my dick, right, Walshy?'

Jimmy ambled around the seminar table. 'I don't get it. Look, we all do a bit of extra work on the side. I write for a magazine. I copy-edit for a PR firm.' Jimmy looked in the mirror. 'I model.' Another glance in the mirror. 'I model a lot. But they've never spoken to me. Are you doing something very public?'

'Never stepped out of the office,' I said.

'You know Indika in the Lower Sixth?' Jimmy asked.

I nodded. 'Teach him econ.'

'His father's the Deputy Minister of Space Programmes.'

'Sri Lanka has a space programme?'

'Not that he's aware of,' Jimmy said. 'But he's in the government and he fixes things like this for us. I can ask him one time, and one time only. You screw up again and you're out.'

'Please, boss, I love it here. Love the school. Love working for you.'

'Okay, stop smelling my farts. We like you too. But keep on the right side of common sense from now on.'

Indika from my Lower Sixth Economics class winked at me. Little shit handed me a note from his father.

Yeah, I got it. He'd done me a favour. Now he'd expect something of me.

I didn't read the note.

I hunted out Mr Samarasekera and asked him why he'd reported me to immigration. He was either a damn good actor or he didn't have a clue what I was on about, and this was a man who could solve most problems.

Back home, I got a text from Jimmy Walsh: 'The Deputy Minister says he sent you a note with the name of the man who reported you to immigration.'

I searched for the trousers I wore during the day and found them in the washing machine. Thankfully, the washing machine didn't work. It rarely did.

Found the note.

The name of the man who reported me to immigration and tried to get me deported?

Thilak Rupasinghe.

seven

When I told Menaka about what her father had done, she looked out of control for the first time. She sped off in her car, almost knocking over a lady who was breastfeeding a malnourished child at the same time as begging for money through car windows.

So again, what little time I had with Menaka had now been lost to something else.

She text-messaged me a few hours later: 'I don't want to talk now. Too bloody angry. Told the old bastard that it's over.'

I could barely breathe. 'What do you mean??? Us?'

She replied: 'No, you jackass. Him and me. I've cut him off. Said I never want to see him again.'

I felt strangely bad about this. 'Okay, whatever you want.'

She messaged: 'We'll stick with the same wedding date, the same plan, the same venue. Will your parents be able to pay?'

Not a hope in hell. 'You know my father's a pastor.'

My phone rang. Screen said Menaka.

'Can you raise some money then?'

'Baba, I earn about a thousand dollars a month at school and I'm not allowed to work for anyone else.'

She hung up. I couldn't believe it, but she hung up.

Moments later, I received a text from her. 'Sorry, baba. Really sorry. That was out of order. This isn't your fault. We'll work something out and all that's important is that we spend our lives together.'

That night she was off at a fundraiser with Gayan; she claimed I wouldn't fit in, but I desperately wanted to be with her and to be part of whatever she was doing.

I could sense, though, that she needed space. I wondered if she still wanted to marry me, even if it was without her dream wedding. She had so many creative ideas for how to perform the most beautiful ceremony ever, and she didn't want to give them to anyone else.

The next day was a public holiday, and despite Menaka's insistence that she was busy, I demanded we meet.

So she took me to the Woman's Institute to help her and a gang of unfashionable fashionistas pack boxes for the IDP camps in the north.

I didn't see nine of the ten ladies touch a box, let alone pack or lift one, and it felt like I was doing all the work because I was. The girls spent most of their time bickering over which organisation they should affiliate themselves to for greatest publicity. When they failed to agree on anything, they took selfies of themselves in front of the boxes, posting them on Facebook with status updates such as, 'The least I could do,' or 'They need us.' These updates garnered replies such as, 'OMG your shoes are amazing.'

The one girl who did any work was a covered Muslim called Hafsa. She kept to herself, but because she was rather frail, I encouraged her not to lift the boxes. Instead, I requested that she record where each box should be sent.

She pointed at Menaka. 'She dated my brother for six months. Talked of marriage, made him turn his back on Islam, on our family. Made him travel the world with her while she dropped out of university after university. Even took the poor guy to Tel Aviv.'

'When was this?' I asked.

'A couple of years ago. Then she dumped him by email from London. Can you believe it?'

Menaka, as if sensing what we were talking about, came over to us and kissed me on the lips, then ambled away with a shaking arse.

'I'm so sorry,' Hafsa said. 'I had absolutely no idea.'

I struggled to say anything because the news didn't really fill me with great hope. 'You weren't to know.'

'Maybe she's changed,' Hafsa said. 'She seems much more settled now.'

I went for a drink with Jimmy Walsh, Robin Hiney and Kenny McAlpine, and in a drunken mess I rambled to myself in the mirror of the Swimming Club gents loo. 'It's just a bit of fun. No marriage, just fun.'

Hangovers are depressing enough, but the next morning I woke up to a message from Menaka. All it said was, 'We need to talk.'

We met at Galle Face Hotel, the oldest establishment east of the Suez. Possibly the most charming too. It first opened in 1864, making it just a fraction older than some of its waiters. We asked one of the octogenarians, Sunil, for a drinks' menu, but we overtook him on the way to the bar and bought our own booze to save time. We ambled down the stairs, a few feet apart, over the black and white squares of the giant chess board, and onto the lawn overlooking the Indian Ocean. As is always the case in Colombo, there were too many people we knew to have an intimate conversation, so we chose a table as far away from the crowd as possible. The choppy waves occasionally crashed into the rock wall below us, spitting seawater across us and into the drinks.

'Does your gin and tonic taste salty?' I asked.

Menaka said nothing, her gaze lost in the grass beneath her Jimmy Choos.

'Shall I make this easier for you?' I leaned across the table and lifted her head up. 'I know what you want to say.'

Her eyes were moist, tears shooting out either side of her face, down her cheeks, into her mouth. She rubbed her eyes with the base of her palms. 'I don't think you do.'

'Everywhere I go, people tell me about your past and –'

'Is that fair?' She took a deep breath, trying to hide that she was about to cry. 'Is it fair for everyone to keep judging me on my past? Is it fair for the one man I love to judge –'

'You love me?' I smiled. If anyone was watching us they would have seen a woman looking miserable and a man looking ecstatic. As if we were watching *Baywatch* or football or some such.

'Of course I love you, Eddie,' she said. 'I wouldn't be marrying you if I didn't.'

'You don't want to call it off?'

She kicked me under the table and smiled, but I didn't. Her Jimmy Choos were sharp.

'Why the hell would I want to call off the wedding?' she asked. 'You're the best damn thing that's ever happened to me.'

I guess it's human nature to be conditioned to believe in something that you know is unlikely to be true, if the lie can, in any way, make you happy. Or less sad, at least. Yet, right then, at that moment, I was convinced that this stunning beauty of a lady was deeply in love with me. That she needed me. That she wanted to live with me for the rest of her life.

Our glasses were empty, but I could see Sunil limping his way down the stairs with our menus, so I remained patient.

'So what do you want to talk about?' I asked.

'You've heard so many negative things about me; it must have had an impact on how you feel.' Her sobbing became more pronounced.

I stood, shielding her from the splashing seawater, bending down to kiss her arms. The smell. Her moisturiser, her natural woman aroma. I said, 'Are you bloody crazy? That's got nothing to do with anything. I mean, what happened before –'

'It has everything to do with everything,' she said. 'You have to tell me if it makes you worry. If it makes you insecure about the marriage.'

'No, I'm –'

'I know it does. But I'm not that person anymore. I'm not the person who is scared of commitment because my mother deserted us; because my father had no time for us till we were grown-ups. I'm not that person.'

I kissed the back of her hands. 'Maybe I'm different.'

'You are,' she said. 'I rushed into other relationships, put too much pressure on myself. They weren't the right men for me.'

'And I am?'

'And you are,' she said.

'So when you said you want to talk –'

'I needed to check you're one hundred per cent sure about the wedding.' She shook her head, her eyes closed. 'Because if you are, I may have to make peace with my father.'

'To pay for the wedding?' I asked.

'No, not just that. Whenever I've dreamed about getting married, that grumpy old bastard has given me away. He has to be there.'

'I think so too.' I got up to help Sunil over the last few yards of the lawn and took the menus from him. 'I think so too.'

eight

We knew that Uncle Thilak was taking the wedding seriously when he sent us to the astrologer. We met a guy in an intricately adorned yellow, high-collared shirt, his hair greased back. He sported a fine moustache, almost too perfectly salt-and-peppered to have been naturally coloured.

His office was air-conditioned and modern, almost clinically so. The astrological charts he had on his wall were framed in mock-gold and lit with electric candles.

He giggled when greeting us, grabbing one of my hands in both of his, not letting go for minutes.

'It is honour for me to be consult for the Thilak Rupasinghe's daughter wedding.'

'Thank you.' Menaka pointed at a chair. 'Shall we sit?'

'Please, please, isit. Isit.' He laughed again. 'You is done this before?'

I shook my head, but tried to feign enthusiasm. 'Never, no.'

'Let me make explain to you. But first, I must tell to you please to not rely only astrology. In Sri Lankan astrology, we uses twenty matching areas called as *porondams* for matching couple birth charts. You understand?'

Not a bloody clue if he was even speaking English. 'Yes, thanks.'

'But it is need for me point out twenty *porondams* or other planets matching are not enough for happy family life. Also must avail yourself of the following: a good family handling skills, like be patient and make a time for said wife.' He looked at Menaka. 'And said husband. Understand?'

She nodded.

'If you are marry you need to stay long time with each of the other. You see?'

'Yes,' I said.

'It is not simple task,' he said. 'Sometimes you make a different choice in life and have a emotional problem.' He looked at Menaka. 'Normally is the woman with emotional. Men is sometimes make a drink, make a cheat, like that, you follow?'

Absolutely no idea what he was saying, so I pulled out the old head wobble.

'Must understand weakness of one and the other and be a kind one.' He held Menaka's hand. 'You see, woman is many time have a ideal how she is want man to live and keep also house clean and not to make the mess. But man sometimes not like that, so please to try to understand you have both different wants. Understand?'

'Yes, uncle,' Menaka said.

'I have check your *porondams*, but you must also consult with parent and elder ones and teachers and also other teachers. Also consult astrologer.' He giggled. 'I am astrologer, no?'

'Yes, indeed,' Menaka said.

'You two is have less matchings than twenty *pornadams*, but your birth charts is have powerful planet combines which is lead to happy family life. You follow?'

He had lost me at hello. 'Yes, I follow.'

'Each *porondam* said some facts about your family life. These are positive ones for the both of you two. For examplar, your *Mahandra porondama* said about family conflicts cause of angry or proud, you see?'

Menaka looked at me. I could see she was biting the inside of her cheeks, trying to suppress laughter. This was contagious and I had to hold a hand to my mouth. I closed my eyes as if I was concentrating, nodded and then lowered my head onto the desk in front of me for a moment.

'Your *Ruksha porondama* said about children and body chemical for parenting. I think you have a nice children, but you cannot rely on what I am only saying. To make a children you must, you know.' He made a crude gesture with his hands, looked at Menaka, raised his eyebrows.

I had to lower my head again, holding my breath so I didn't lose control. Menaka took a sip of water.

'Your *Graha porondama* said about how each other's lovely attraction to family life.'

Menaka went first, water bursting out of her mouth past her glass. I had never seen her laugh so much, and, in turn, I lost it completely. At the same time, I tried to dab tissues on the astrologer's shirt to dry the water Menaka had spat at him accidentally.

He joined in the laughter, fortunately. 'Oh, I tell you, this is a funny one, more funnier than other funny ones I am have in this office. I think you are make a nervous and thusfore the water is come fly from inside your mouth.'

'Your shirt,' Menaka tried to say. 'I will pay to have it dry-cleaned.'

'Can you give us a second, sir?' I asked. 'We need to go outside for a second to calm ourselves down.'

'This is I understand. It is big moment in this life of yours two.'

꒰ ꒱

It took us almost fifteen minutes to gather our composure.

We knew we were being incredibly disrespectful. Sure, maybe we didn't believe in this stuff, but a lot of people did and this mustachioed guru was the most sought-after practitioner of them all. So, hands held up in prayer, heads bowed, we re-entered his office.

'This is so helpful,' Menaka said. 'Please, can you continue?'

He looked angry for a moment, then broke out into a wonderful, white smile. '*Varna porondama* is said about each of yours unique skills need for the family life such as cooking talent, talking talent, loving and the etcetera. This is good.'

'Happy to hear,' I said, holding my breath so I was not sure if any words came out.

'*Nadi porondama* said about each partner's body condition for the cure of sickness such as a chemical complex.' He leaned forward and held Menaka's wrists. 'This is remind to me, how is your father and his cancer, he is cure no?'

'Yes, he's cured,' she said.

The astrologer nodded. 'Yes, I told to him he is cure soon. But please to warn him, he cannot rely on me only to tell to him. He must keep to himself in the good health, make a not drink, make a not smoke. Correct?'

'Correct,' she said.

'Otherwise, sure to get the cancer again. Sure to die.'

On the way home we were silent. The belief in astrology was, to each of us, about as alien as Scientology. Neither of us believed in voodoo either, but if I saw a long-haired, war-painted guy by a fire with an Eddie doll he was just about to stick pins into, I'd try to stop him. It plays on your mind. Hell, even when someone says they dreamed about you in a car crash, you start driving more carefully.

So when we got back to Uncle Thilak, Menaka surprised both of us by hugging him tighter and for longer than normal. He looked over her shoulder, mouthing to me, 'What's wrong with her?'

'Thathi.' Menaka leaned out of the hug. 'The astrologer said you have to take care of yourself.'

'You were supposed to see him about your marriage,' Uncle Thilak said.

'Yes, yes, we did, but he mentioned that you can't drink or smoke or you'll suffer again.'

Uncle Thilak laughed. 'I thought you didn't believe in this stuff.'

'I don't, but –'

'Said it was Colombo Mumbo Jumbo.'

'But still, Thathi, just be careful.'

Uncle Thilak patted her on the shoulder. 'Your marriage to a *suddha* is more likely to be the death of me than a few drinks and cigarettes.'

nine

My mother went silent on the phone when I told her I was getting married to someone she had never even heard about. Yet, my parents loved me enough to accept my choice and to fly out for the wedding. They hadn't even seen pictures of Menaka, which was as planned because I wanted to surprise them with how beautiful she was. My father, a former military pastor, handled all religious affairs for the Royal Chelsea Hospital at the time. This meant they lived in a five thousand square foot house off King's Road, albeit within the hospital grounds, but they didn't have much ready cash. They were saving to come out to visit me in Sri Lanka anyway, but I doubt they would have thought of doing so with wedding kit in tow.

Menaka and I wanted to pick them up from the airport, but Uncle Thilak insisted that he should. 'This is my country and they are my guests,' he said.

He borrowed, from a friend, the Rolls Royce that transported Queen Elizabeth II around when she visited Sri Lanka in 1954 and it turned out to be fitting because my father looked enough like Prince Charles to con a few people into assuming he was on a royal visit.

Menaka and I waited for their arrival at the Cinnamon Grand, where Uncle Thilak had booked them a two-bedroom suite. Because they were greeted at the hotel by Kandyan drummers and an elephant, some of the guests assumed my father was the heir to the English throne, something he played up to by clasping his hands behind his back and stooping forward ever so slightly to address people.

Mum hugged me while Dad ruffled my hair, both backing away to greet Menaka.

'Oh dear,' said Dad, 'she's far too good for my boy.'

Uncle Thilak nodded so much his comb-over flicked out of place. 'That's what I've been telling him.'

'Cheers, Papa,' I said. 'Uncle Thilak.'

Menaka dipped her head a little, playing the part of the humble Asian wife, not letting on that she was very much the sarong-wearer in our relationship.

'You're absolutely stunning.' My mother beamed, smiling so much her eyes closed, squeezing tears out. 'My little boy has really landed on his feet here.'

'What's the secret?' Dad asked. 'Why on earth are you marrying him?'

'I've questioned her every day,' Uncle Thilak said.

Mum kissed my cheek and hung onto my right arm. 'Darling, I'm so proud of you. The most beautiful girl in the world, and her father is utterly charming.'

'Thank you, madam,' Uncle Thilak said.

'You're marrying into such a warm family.'

'And a brainy one,' Dad said. 'Thilak is a genius. You'll have smart kids, I imagine. Much smarter than you, at least.'

'You're making me blush with your fatherly praise,' I said.

The next day, Uncle Thilak took my parents on a tour of Colombo, after which they travelled five hours to the centre of the island, meeting us at Kandalama Hotel just before midnight. Mum and Dad looked like they had seen a ghost, but Sri Lankan roads can do that to you. I had to share their room because there wasn't a fat chance in hell Uncle Thilak would have approved of me bunking up with Menaka before we were married. Regardless, it was a joy to see how happy and relaxed my parents were to wake up overlooking the man-made lake.

We joined the Rupasinghes for breakfast. There were counters for egg hoppers, *kothu rothi*, eggs, waffles, fresh fruit. All things we took for granted, but that my parents salivated over. Outside, a grass deck overlooked the lake, the hills and all the greenery, as exotic birds tweeted around us.

'Paradise,' my father said. 'So fresh.'

Uncle Thilak didn't look fresh. His eyes were virtually closed, the bags under them puffed up like bean bags.

A waiter placed a pot of tea next to him. He looked up and gave him a warm, but crooked smile.

'Thank you, Sunil,' he said.

Menaka waited till the waiter was out of earshot. 'His name's not Sunil.'

'If in doubt, call them Sunil,' he said to my father. 'The majority of waiters in this country are called Sunil.'

Menaka poured his tea and sprinkled it with four sachets of sugar.

He sipped from it, spat what he had in his mouth back into the cup and grabbed the waiter's arm as he walked past. 'What the hell is this?'

Mum held my wrist under the table, clearly shaken by the change in Uncle Thilak's tone.

The waiter turned and said, 'Tea, sir.'

'But it's boiling hot, you stupid donkey. Scorching.'

'Yes, sir,' the waiter said. 'It's tea.'

'Call the manager, you idiot.'

He managed to keep his voice low enough to blend in with the murmuring of tourists and the clattering of cutlery.

'I've been coming here for ten years,' he said to the manager. 'So you should know by now that I like my tea warm, not hot.'

'Did he serve you hot tea?' The manager bent forward at the waist, holding his hands together.

'Do you want to see the inside of my mouth?' Uncle Thilak said. 'I can't have things that hot.'

'He's new, sir.'

'And he's a damn idiot. I never want to see him here again.'

'You want me to sack him, sir?'

Uncle Thilak shook his head. 'No, no, don't go so far. Just send him to the other side of the restaurant.'

My mother jabbed at the pineapple on her plate, probably too stunned to know what to say until the Rupasinghes left the table. 'It must be the cancer,' she said later. 'He went through so much. I think it's just made him a little on edge.'

'Quite jolting really,' Dad said. 'I can see why you're scared of him, Eddie.'

A storm began to brew when we were halfway up Sigiriya, climbing the metal staircase on the way to the ruins of a palace built on top of a six-hundred-and-sixty foot rock. The wind whistled around us, shaking wasps off their hives and into the paths of the tourists. Although this was his country, his world, it was Uncle Thilak who looked the most concerned about the weather. Aiya and I helped him up the stairs, holding up pretty much everyone else: foreigners, school kids, even a few monks.

My mother was deep in conversation with Menaka about the IDP work that she did and pledged to donate two hundred pounds for dry rations. This was a huge amount in my mother's mind, a pittance to Menaka, but I was glad they were bonding. They had already been out shopping together and had beauty treatments and fit-ons, lattes and oysters.

My father stood behind us, in ridiculous red trousers and a wide-rimmed hat, as if he was there to catch Uncle Thilak if he were to fall, but all he did was speak very loudly about what a brilliant bowler Muttiah Muralitharan was.

We scaled the final stairway, a giant lion's claws erected on either side of the first few steps.

'Look down, *suddha*,' Uncle Thilak said to me. 'Impressive, no?'

'Very.'

He turned to my father. 'Your son refused to come with me to see this site. Can you believe that?'

'He's never been inquisitive,' my father said. 'Bless him, for that is my job.'

The breeze stiffened, so we moved to sit on a solid rock-step away from the crowd. A man tried to sell us bottles of warm soft drinks for ten times the market price. The sun began to dip within an expanse of greenery and mud paths. Mum, Dad and I ambled away from the others and made sure that we explored every inch of the summit.

'An amazing man.' My father put his hands behind his back, closed his eyes and tucked his chin into his chest. 'A tad intimidating, but amazing. You should write a book about him. How he fought cancer, how he fought against injustice.'

'Good sense of humour too,' Mum said.

'He's just charming you,' I said. 'He's not always like this.'

'Thilak,' Dad said, beckoning him over with his hand. That was not a good idea at all – not a good idea for the average person, but for *Thilak Rupasinghe* to be summoned by a *white man*! Oh dear.

Much to my surprise, Uncle Thilak limped towards my father.

Dad gave me his hat and then patted his hair down into a Prince Charles hairstyle. He clasped his hands behind his back then marched around the edge of the rock.

'Watch this, Thilak.'

It took a few moments for the odd person, first a school kid, then a German tourist, then a monk, to point at him.

'He's pretending to be Prince Charles,' I said.

'No shit,' Uncle Thilak said. 'They're not really falling for it.'

'Dad's trying so hard not to laugh,' Mum said. 'This is his standard party trick.'

My father took out his mobile phone and moved closer to the German, the school kid and the monk.

'Mummy,' he said into the phone, his accent Eton posh. 'I'm in Sri Lanka...you know the place south of India...no that's Australia. I mean the place that your great-great-great-great-great-grandpapa George colonised and plundered? Yes that's the one...yes lovely tea...well, I am standing on top of Sigiriya...it's a palace on a giant rock...well that's why I'm calling, Mummy, I want it... No, not something like it, I want this one. I have to have it. No no no, mummy please, come on, it's no fair. I want it. I want...hello, hello. She hung up on me. Can you believe it?'

My mother dipped her head into her hands. 'So embarrassing.'

Luckily, Menaka and Aiya laughed, which made my father strut back to us like a boxer about to enter the ring.

I turned to see if Uncle Thilak was amused, but he suddenly looked like a South Indian movie villain: nose scrunched up, eyes small, left fist wrenched in right hand.

No, he wasn't amused.

Back at Kandalama Hotel, I sat on Mum and Dad's balcony,

mere feet away from a monkey wedged between two branches, munching on a mango.

Mum and Dad looked so content. Sun-burnt, jaded, but content. They didn't have the energy to speak to me and I didn't have the energy to speak to them, so we soaked in each other's vibes in silence, like all those many years at the breakfast table while I was still sponging off them. At dinner, my father used to say, 'Conversation is overrated,' and then talk all night. Crack jokes. Check if we were laughing. Back then I knew they worried about me. I had been a top student and sportsman at school, but university made me lazy. My parents often told me my life lacked direction and I only took up accountancy to try to prove that I could make something of myself. Then I packed it in when I realised how much I had to study and their worries grew.

Till they met Menaka.

I watched my father smiling as he sucked in the fresh Kandalama lake air. I heard my Mum hum in tune with the monkeys and birds and I knew they were proud of me.

We had drinks with the Rupasinghes by an infinity pool, elevated on a hill. It had become too dark to take in the view, but under the half moon, the reflection off the man-made lake made us feel like we were in the stars.

The topic of conversation swayed to Britain's colonisation of Sri Lanka and my mother said all the right things to win Uncle Thilak's favour.

My father, on the other hand, kept saying how we had given the country cricket, rugby, roads and railways. I was surprised, and somewhat touched, that Uncle Thilak didn't argue against this. He was making an effort to get on with the parents of his daughter's future husband. I had a sneaky feeling, though, that the more he drank, the more likely his patience would snap.

He must have had at least seven arracks by the time he called for the bill.

As soon as he did, my father excused himself and went to the loo. This was a habit of his, and a rather embarrassing one. In his old age his pockets seemed to be getting deeper and his arms shorter.

The waiter left the bill on the table and I wanted to take it and sign it to our room, worrying about how I would actually pay for it later. I had no idea how whopping it would be and I knew I couldn't look at it and then reject it.

Still, I had to do what I had to do. I reached out to grab it but Uncle Thilak used his walking stick to nudge my hand away.

'I want to see how long your old man hides for,' he said.

Mum stretched out a bit to see if she could see where Dad was.

'Just pay the bill, Thathi,' Menaka said.

Uncle Thilak looked towards the Gents, then down at his watch. 'He's been in there for eight minutes already.'

'Thathi, please,' Menaka said. 'Please.'

'It's a matter of principle. Nine minutes now.'

'Let me get that,' Mum said, reaching for the bill.

Uncle Thilak got to it before her. 'No, I could never allow a lady to pay.'

I looked at my watch. 'I'll go see if Dad's okay. Maybe he slipped.'

'Stay where you are,' Uncle Thilak said, his speech slurring.

'Shall I take you to the room, Thathi?' Menaka asked.

Uncle Thilak shook his head. 'Get me another drink. I'm going to charge it to that cheap bastard anyway.'

'Thathi –'

'Get me another bloody drink.'

My mother jumped in her chair, her hands flapping.

Menaka turned to me. 'Baba, take your Mum and Dad to your room. I'm so, so sorry.'

'Mum, come on,' I said. 'I'll get Dad.'

'Where is that cheap white prick?' Uncle Thilak held Menaka's wrist. 'That bugger hasn't even offered to pay a cent towards anything since he's been here. Not even his own bloody ticket at Sigiriya.'

I ran towards the Gents and found Dad sticking his head around the door to see what was happening.

'Has the bill been paid yet?' he asked.

I lay on the extra bed with the lights off. I knew Mum and Dad were still awake because if they weren't there would have been an orchestra of snoring.

I think Dad felt a little shame at being rumbled for being cheap, but above all they were shocked at Uncle Thilak's outburst. And it hadn't stopped there. We could hear him shouting from his room next door for another couple of hours, but thankfully we couldn't understand what he was saying through the walls.

I woke up to a message from Menaka asking me to tell her when we were all awake so that she could come talk to us. I poured her a tea and she joined my parents on their balcony.

'I simply can't apologise enough for last night,' she said. 'There's no excuse, I know, but he's not always like that.'

'Are you okay?' my mother asked. 'He seemed to be going at you and your brother all night.'

'We're used to it. We switch off. Nothing else we can do, really, except try to keep him away from other people when he's like that.'

'It's not my place to ask,' my mother said, 'but is he always like that when he drinks?'

'You're worried about serving alcohol at the wedding?'

Mum nodded.

'He drinks all the time, so no.' Menaka wiped a tear out of her eye. I think it was a real one. 'Since he got cancer he's had episodes like this. Not often, but when they happen...' She bowed her head.

My mother put an arm around her.

'When they happen we just have to bear with him. There's no reasoning.'

'How's he today?' I asked.

'As if nothing happened.'

'But we decided already,' my father said, 'that we better head off early today to avoid him.'

'I understand,' Menaka said. 'You can get a hotel cab and put it on his bill.'

'Thank you. And what room numb –'

'Dad, no.'

ten

Menaka's friends arrived from Australia with typical Bondi Beach, *Home and Away* type names: Aman, Zubin, Aida, Fatema, Ali, Mohammed, Deepak, Dev and Kapil.

I stayed the last couple of nights before the wedding with my parents in their suite. We had a good time in a simple kind of way: room service, lots of cakes, pirated DVDs, hot chocolates. But it was impossible not to notice that Mum and Dad's enthusiasm had taken a huge hit. In its place was acceptance that their son was marrying the daughter of a man they wouldn't get on with.

'Are you sure about this?' Dad asked me.

I didn't answer. I just smiled. I knew, at the heart of it, Dad wanted me to get married to Menaka. He was very fond of her. Yet, there was no coming back for his relationship with Uncle Thilak and I could understand why. What he had to realise was that I was signing up to spend my life with Menaka, not Uncle Thilak. I would promise to be with her, in sickness and in health, and if we had children, I'd bring them up with Menaka, not him.

The astrologer instructed me that the auspicious time to leave the hotel on the day of the wedding was 6.23 a.m. The ceremony was at lunchtime so Gayan and I, dressed in our wedding gear, cruised around in the Jag – me in a gold kurta, brown collar, brown shawl, and Gayan in a black suit. We smoked some smokes, drank some beer. He was on the phone with Menaka most of the time. Whispering. Giggling.

We arrived at the Hilton. Kandyan dancers led me onto the *poruwa* stand: a wooden platform decorated with *punkalas*, clay oil lamps, jasmine, grains of rice and *pori*. The dancers began to drum, leaping, circling. Menaka was by my side: gold sari; jewellery in her hair, down her neck, her ears. My family and Gayan on the left of the *poruwa*. Menaka and family on the right.

I greeted her with palms held together.

The MC presented a handful of betel leaves to us. We passed it straight back to him as if he was a baby who couldn't quite relinquish his toys. He placed the leaves on the height of the *poruwa*. 'The offering of betel to the gods,' he whispered to me in English, between his high-pitched Sinhala chanting.

Uncle Thilak put Menaka's right hand on mine.

Gayan passed me a tray with seven sheaves of betel leaves, a coin placed on each, the coin worth about two pence. I held the tray as instructed. Menaka took a sheaf and dropped it on the *poruwa* like a petulant child, but that's apparently what she was meant to do.

We repeated this seven times, to remember seven generations of relatives on each side.

Dad shrugged his shoulders and breathed out a little too loudly. Mum nudged him and reminded him to hand me a gold chain which I draped around Menaka's neck. All my savings plus some loans.

Gehan, Uncle Thilak's cousin, tied my small finger to Menaka's with gold thread and then poured water over it.

'Water and earth being the eternal verities,' the MC said in English for my benefit. Shouldn't have bothered as I had no idea what he meant. 'The water so poured and the earth on which it falls are intended to be the lasting witness to the marriage.'

'I'll have whatever he's smoking,' my father said. Too loud.

Gehan then turned us clockwise three times.

I presented Menaka with a white cloth which she gave to her aunt, because her mother had absconded so many years ago. Abandoned them. Menaka could have cried at this point but she didn't, perhaps backing up my theory that she only ever cried fake tears.

'That is an expression of your gratitude for bringing up your bride,' the MC said.

Cheap gratitude, I thought.

The aunt handed me a sari.

'That's for me to wear,' Menaka said. 'Going away sari. Don't worry, we're nearly done.'

'Loving it,' I said.

Uncle Thilak pointed his fingers at me like a gun, just before Menaka and I infected each other with our giggles.

Aunty presented a plate of milk rice and *kavum* to Menaka who fed a piece of each to me. One was nice, one disgusting – the good cop, bad cop of Sri Lankan wedding ceremony food.

I fed Menaka.

The MC broke a coconut in two. At the third attempt.

We lit a brass oil lamp, then sat at a table.

'This is all we really need to do,' Menaka said.

Finally, we signed the registry.

One thousand nine hundred and fifty wedding guests clapped the new husband and wife.

Yet, I felt as if this had nothing to do with me, like I was a mere guest at a massive Rupasinghe party.

My parents hugged me, a resigned look on their faces like when I first left for Sri Lanka.

'You're always welcome at home, okay?' Mum's tears slalomed down her wrinkled face.

'You've done your bit.' Taru hugged me, and since she is the best wedding planner in the world, this reassured me. 'Now all you have to do is smile, and I'll do everything else.' She offered me one of her cigarettes, but Menaka slapped my hand away just before I accepted it.

Champagne corks popped. The ballroom opened. The budget for flowers was higher than the overall budget for most weddings. The food cost two hundred and fifty dollars a plate. That's two month's salary for Uncle Thilak's maids.

We posed for about nineteen thousand permutations and combinations of pictures. Menaka with me, Menaka with me and my parents, Menaka with me and her family. Menaka and me, and our two fathers. Menaka and me and my mother and her aunt. Menaka and me and a picture of her dead grandfather. Menaka and Uncle Thilak with the same picture. Uncle Thilak and me with the picture. The picture alone. The picture in profile. The picture kissing another picture.

We ate one-tenth of our two-hundred-and-fifty dollar plate. Twenty-five dollars worth. Then Uncle Thilak paraded us around the hall, while people I'd never seen before leapt out to congratulate us. Or some, like the President of the country, I had seen before but not met.

Menaka had told Uncle Thilak again and again that we wanted speeches to be 'like Sri Lankan men. Short and sweet.' Maybe he got the memo, but he didn't pass it onto the other speakers.

The Attorney General spoke for eighteen minutes, using almost every Internet wedding joke out there.

The Chief Justice lectured us about the legal obligations we had signed up to.

Three other people spoke. Even Menaka had no idea who they were.

Menaka's bridesmaid, who flew in from the States, addressed the audience in some bogus American accent that contained too many 'I's. I did this with Menaka. I did this to be here. I told her to get married. I want to get married soon. I am like, so awesome.

The guests barely noticed speeches were being made. Lots of '*how, how, machangs*', lots of 'you've put on', lots of 'you've gone down'.

No one listened, till Uncle Thilak got to the podium.

Murmurs. Shooooosh. Shooosh. It's him.

They wiped tears out of their eyes when he spoke. His own tears reflected the lights. The great little man. The feared little man.

A beautiful speech about Menaka, but he didn't mention marriage once.

Didn't mention my family once.

Didn't mention me once.

Part II

eleven

When I need to feel macho I imagine myself applying warpaint onto my face, loading my ammo, locking a revolver into my holster, polishing my Bowie knife.

This, however, is my reality:

Four scoops of formula powder in a functional dispenser.

An Avent baby bottle with four ounces of boiled water.

A BPA free plastic container filled with strawberry yoghurt snacks.

Mosquito patch on Kiki's back.

Mosquito repellent on Kiki's arms and legs.

Drape the Baby Bjorn over my shoulders.

Lift Kiki into the Baby Bjorn, facing out to keep her stimulated.

Fasten all straps.

Lift up baby bag.

Exit house.

The same thing everyday.

Kiki is almost a year old now. She was born the day the civil war ended, and less than nine months after our wedding. My mother flew out to help us for the first couple of weeks, but since then, it's been just me, although Uncle Thilak helps when he can. Menaka has very little time for Kiki. Honourably, or not, her time is taken up by more high-profile pursuits involving post-war reconciliation. This is what she wanted to do. She had always set out to be there, a guiding light, ultimately a historical figure in Sri Lanka's new age. An age of uniting the races and moving forward into the twenty-first century.

Besides, being a stay-at-home-mum wouldn't get her on TV.

Uncle Thilak gave us fifty perches of land in Thalawathugoda, on a former rubber estate. We live next door to this land in a rented house overlooking the paddy fields, waiting for construction to finish.

Construction that Uncle Thilak is paying for.

Kiki falls asleep even though facing out of the Bjorn, so I visit the site.

I pull the foreman by the ear. Uncle Thilak says if you treat people nicely here, they'll take the piss.

'What the hell is this?' I point at a bathtub.

'It's a bathtub.' He rifles through a file to a picture I have signed off on. 'This is the bathtub you approve. You approve this one. I have your autograph.' His speech gets higher and higher. 'You approve this one.'

'But this is the kitchen. Why the hell have you installed it here?'

'Ah, this is kitchen, no?' he says. 'Aiyo, sir, sorry, sir. You want me to move it to the bathroom?'

'Yes, I want you to move this luxury bathtub out of the kitchen.'

It's like this every day. Kiki and me on site visits. Menaka at work. Work she couldn't do until the war ended.

The timing is terrible. Menaka has a new life, networking and finding the right outlets and channels to make the greatest impact, you know, like, to the world. For example, today I imagine she will have a late meeting at Coffee Bean with some highly paid expat NGO workers who live in houses with swimming pools. If not, she'll go to Water's Edge for a swim or a weights session. I doubt she'll be home before I get Kiki to sleep. It's become such a norm that she no longer makes any effort to race back before bedtime, even if it means she has to go out again after.

This is why I had to quit my job.

This is why I am a regular at kids' play areas, Jitterbug classes and baby groups.

*

I take Kiki for her one year jabs a few days early because Uncle Thilak wants to take us all away this weekend. I've packed my bag and Kiki's. I haven't bothered with Menaka's as she will cancel at the last minute.

Dr Farij tells me that Kiki will not get a temperature from these jabs. I tell Uncle Thilak this, but he still gives her Panadol and rubs cologne on her head. I argue with him about this. It pisses me off intensely when he does these things to my baby. Like when he had a monk light incense in Kiki's room while he 'chanted away her cholic'.

But at least he cares about her. At least he loves her. At least he accepts his responsibility to her.

So when Menaka calls to say that she is not coming home tonight, I agree to Uncle Thilak's suggestion to go out and let off some steam. I trust him to put Kiki to bed.

'No sheets and pillows, uncle.'

I go for a run up to JoJo's house for a beer. About two-hundred-and-thirty pounds, long beard, side parting, JoJo's a tea taster and self-proclaimed 'good eating, drinking bugger'. We eat and drink, but don't bugger.

I stumble home after a long session, check in on Kiki and want to slam the door. Uncle Thilak has put her to bed with pillows.

It's 2 a.m., but I text him.

He replies at 2.02. 'She's too old now to get suffocated by pillows.'

I know he's right, but still. Kiki is my bloody baby. Why can't he just listen to me?

I wake to a text from Menaka. 'Babe, I'll have to cancel this weekend. Too much on my plate. You and Kiki go with Thathi. How is my little angel?'

As if she gives a shit. So I lie. 'She's got a high temperature.'

Giving my baby fake illnesses to attract attention from my wife could be tempting fate. What am I doing?

She doesn't reply.

I drive to the Lighthouse Hotel in Galle; Uncle Thilak's in the back with Kiki. He sings badly. Very badly. His repertoire includes all the old classic nursery rhymes, but none of the right lyrics.

Yet I like him singing, because it stops him from bitching about my driving: 'You turned too sharp, almost hit that bus.' 'Are you trying to kill your baby?' 'Aiyo, aiyo, overtake that bloody trishaw.'

For an old man and former cancer patient, he displays surprising agility when he leans over my shoulder to beep the horn because he thinks the bullock cart in front of us is not making any effort to get out of the way.

Inevitably, Kiki cries. I suggest that she is frustrated being tied up in her seat for too long and that maybe we should stop and let her crawl around on the beach.

'Nonsense,' Uncle Thilak says. 'Bloody hungry, that's all.'

He digs into the baby bag and brings out the formula milk powder.

'Not a good idea, uncle,' I say. 'Might make her throw up.'

'What bloody cock, *suddha*.' He laughs. 'This is milk, not arrack.' He begins to mix the formula powder with the water.

Looking in the rear-view mirror, I almost crash into the back of a motorcycle carrying an off-duty policeman and his three little children. None in helmets.

'Uncle, if she doesn't want it, it'll be wasted. We have to use it within an hour of mixing.'

He raises his palm. 'Just drive, you bugger. You worry about getting us there, I'll worry about keeping this baby happy.' He sticks the bottle in Kiki's mouth and, to his credit, she stops crying. In the mirror, I can see from her cheeks how hard she is sucking. She must be very hungry.

The problem is, Uncle Thilak is an old-timer, and old-timers in this country hate to waste. It's pretty obvious Kiki doesn't want the last couple of ounces, but Uncle Thilak keeps wedging the teat in her mouth. She tries to flap it away with her hands, but Uncle Thilak is in a race against his watch. I wish I had not reminded him of the one-hour-formula rule.

'She's had enough,' I say.

'Stick to your lane, *suddha*,' he says. 'Swerving the car too much.'

'Look, she's trying to push you away.'

'Keep your bloody eyes on the road. Terrible bloody drivers you white people are. Almost as bad as Muslims and those buggers have to worry about their beards getting tangled in the steering wheel.'

A gagging noise precedes Kiki throwing up – milk, beetroot, whole strawberries – through her mouth, gunk through her nose, up against the back of the passenger's seat, all over her clothes.

Silence.

Kiki surveys the scene, then screams so loudly she drowns out the sounds of street dogs and musical bus horns.

My tyres screech as I swerve across the road almost onto the beach. I jump out of the car, get to the back and pull Kiki out. I push her head down onto my shoulder, the smell of vomit almost overwhelming me. 'It's okay, it's okay, Daddy's here.'

Uncle Thilak pokes his head out of the car. 'Don't worry baba, Seeya's here.'

'I told you not to give her milk,' I say.

'It's not the milk, you white jackass. It was your bloody sickening driving. I almost threw up myself.'

'Just help me.' I hold Kiki under the armpits. She giggles. 'Pull the trousers off.'

'Bet lots of men said that to you at that bloody gay English boarding school of yours.'

'Not the time, uncle.'

He pulls the trousers off and hurls them on the roof of the car. Between us, we manage to strip Kiki down to her nappy, but now she is howling again, likely thirsty, or hungry, and we have nothing to give her.

'My kids never cried,' Uncle Thilak says. 'She must have got that from your side.'

꒦꓇꙰

We pull into the Lighthouse Hotel, its burnt orange exterior a homage to Galle's Dutch heritage. I climb the spiral staircase to the reception with a crying, half-naked baby and a cantankerous bald git in sandals and white socks.

We stink of vomit.

Uncle Thilak has booked only one room for us, which I would rectify if I had any money of my own. The room is amazing.

Wooden floors, turquoise window frames, walk-in closet. I'd much rather be sharing this with Menaka than her old man.

While I swim with Kiki, Uncle Thilak takes off his shirt and has a beer and a smoke on the wooden sun-deck surrounded by green foliage, above the rocks that lead into the sea.

In the pool, a little Dutch boy points at the dip and scar on Uncle Thilak's neck. The boy makes a yuck face and hugs his mother, who appears to tell him off before making a yuck face herself.

Another woman approaches me. She's maybe twenty-seven or so, hot as the chilli Uncle Thilak tries to poison me with. 'So cute.' She strokes Kiki's hair.

Kiki doesn't cry, which is a good sign, even though she's started to get a bit clingy.

The woman tells me her name, but I don't catch it, because Uncle Thilak is shouting from the pool bar, 'He's married, lady, don't waste your time.'

I want to throw my head under water, but I have Kiki in my arms.

The lady tries to tell me her name again.

'This isn't Europe, you know,' Uncle Thilak says. 'Married men don't sleep with other women here. Unless they pay, and this beggar son-in-law of mine has no money.'

The lady's freestyle kicks water on my face and gets chlorine in Kiki's eyes. She's out of the pool before I can say I'm sorry. I try to give Uncle Thilak the meanest look I have, but he just laughs. Annoyingly, so does Kiki.

We take Kiki for a walk on the beach. The waves scare the shit out of her, quite literally, forcing me to change her nappy. Uncle Thilak gives me instructions all the way through this, primarily about not wasting the wipes. He doesn't offer any help until after I've finished. Kiki stands and we hold one of her hands each. Uncle Thilak keeps her on the side where he does not have a hole in his neck.

One, two, three – we swing her so her legs flap forward and back, and she giggles. 'Agga,' she says. 'Agga.'

Uncle Thilak, for the hundredth time, claims 'agga' means 'again' in Sinhala, but I checked this with Menaka a week ago and it's rubbish.

But we do it again.

One, two, three, swing.

'Must give her curry for dinner.'

One, two, three, swing.

'She's only one,' I say. 'Her mouth will catch fire.'

One, two, three, swing.

'Bloody nonsense, you bugger. She's not a white girl, you know.' Uncle Thilak stops walking and swinging. 'You married a brown girl and you live in a brown country. Don't bring her up white.'

Kiki cries.

One, two, three, swing.

'I'm embracing your culture,' I say.

'You're embarrassing my culture,' he says.

One, two, three, swing.

'Making her look like a bloody boy,' he says.

'She's wearing pink.'

One, two, three, swing.

Uncle Thilak shouts, 'But no bloody earrings. Pierce her bloody ears, you bugger.'

'She's too young.'

'Oh yes, you want to wait until she can make the choice for herself.' He's mocking my accent. 'That's so democratic of you. Why not wait till she can make the choice about changing nappies too?'

One, two, three, swing.

The bickering continues. Couples strolling in the other direction swivel in the sand as they pass us, saying 'sweet' with their smiles.

Two men, with a beautiful baby.

At dinner, on a slight cliff above the sea, while Kiki's asleep in her pram, a couple from Norway praises us for bringing up a girl so well together. They think we're gay dads. My main concern is that they didn't acknowledge the age difference.

Either Uncle Thilak does not understand the insinuation or he finds it amusing.

It's our last day at the Lighthouse, and Uncle Thilak sits, fully dressed, on the edge of the pool, with his trousers rolled up. His legs dangle into the water up to his shins.

I get a text from Menaka asking how the trip is going. She doesn't specifically ask about her baby.

I push Kiki in her pram until she falls asleep, her hair blowing in the sea breeze. I get myself a beer, light a smoke and look out to the sea. Oh, the bliss. The relaxation. The condensation on the beer bottle making the label stick to my hand. The smoke tasting vaguely salty. I close my eyes.

Suddenly, I hear a big splash and open my eyes.

Uncle Thilak's in the water, flapping his arms about.

He can't swim.

I'm torn. Save him, but take my eyes off Kiki. Or just stay with Kiki.

I don't have to make the decision because a German tourist gets to Uncle Thilak before the Sri Lankan lifeguard. Both pull him out.

Uncle Thilak points at me. 'He pushed me in.'

I smile. It's quite a funny accusation, I must say.

He smiles too, for my benefit, but his acting continues for the others. 'My son-in-law pushed me in because I asked if I could have another papaya juice. *Sin*, no?'

Later in the car on the way home, I get my revenge by pointing out that, again, a Sri Lankan was saved by a white man. This, of course, sparks an intense argument about how the Germans are much better at everything than the English.

I can't argue when he gets onto the topic of penalties.

twelve

On the 16th of May 2009, the President of Sri Lanka, addressing the G11 summit in Jordan, said, 'My government, with the total commitment of our armed forces, has in an unprecedented humanitarian operation finally defeated the LTTE militarily.'

Around this time, Menaka was in labour and on pethidine to ease the pain of Kiki's impending birth.

She had complained of slight cramps the night before, but we waited till daybreak to take her into Joseph Fraser Memorial Hospital to check whether this was the time.

And it was. Menaka, rare for her, looked completely and utterly powerless. She asked a million questions of the nurses and kept calling the doctor to ask him when he would be there. She seemed scared, not so much of the untold pain, but more by the lack of control she had in it all.

'Kiki's the boss now, I guess,' she said.

'She'll come out when she's good and ready.'

The nurses asked me to leave the room when they wanted to give Menaka an enema. I could see in her big eyes the worry, the sadness, that I would not be with her for this short phase. Never had I felt so wanted.

Then on pethidine, she was dopey in the labour room. Her eyes opened and closed involuntarily. I tried to tell her about the war ending but she didn't seem to take it in.

The nurses kept checking her cervical dilation but it wasn't happening fast enough. Then the pethidine wore off. Menaka squeezed my hand, begging me to make them give her more but they said it was too soon for a second dose.

The doctor dropped by, looking like he didn't have a care in the world. In fact, looking like he had never had a care in his life.

'The war's over,' he said.

Menaka's eyes bulged open. She pumped her fist in the air and then grimaced. 'Please, just give me a bloody C-section.'

The doctor checked her dilation again. 'Need to induce,' he said. 'Bugger should be out in an hour or two.'

'Pain relief?' I asked.

'Wait, wait, we'll give more.' He ripped off his rubber gloves. 'I told you it's a boy, no?'

'You said girl,' I said.

'It better be a bloody girl,' Menaka said. 'Her room's pink.'

'I thought boy.' He rubbed his bald head.

'A ladyboy?' I said.

The doctor slapped his own leg, bent over himself laughing. 'Ladyboy, I tell you man.'

'Come here, come here, come here,' Menaka said. She dug her nails into the back of his hand. 'Give me an epidural, please.'

'Can't, can't, you have to push.'

'Just focus on your breathing,' I said. 'Then it won't hurt.'

The doctor laughed. 'That's some new age bloody nonsense. Yesterday had a woman lighting candles all around the room. Had music, had scents. English-speaking, posh lady, pretended she couldn't even speak Sinhala. Baby started coming, she blurted out every bloody Sinhala swear word there is.'

'This isn't helping,' Menaka said.

The doctor rubbed his head again. 'I used to have a lot of hair, but these women pulled it out.'

'I hope you have some tactic here, doctor,' I said. 'You're just making her more anxious.'

'It's bloody painful. No way around it, so you just have to concentrate on pushing when you have contractions. Can't waste them. The better you do this, the faster it will be over.'

He was almost out the door when Menaka screamed. 'Doctor, doctor.'

He came back into the room and plopped a stool next to her.

'Just tell me one thing,' Menaka said. 'Is Prabhakaran dead?'

The doctor returned an hour later in a raincoat and wellington boots. 'For the blood,' he said.

'Again, not so reassuring,' I said.

Menaka didn't even see him. The pain was too much for her to open her eyes. 'C-section, please, please.'

'Her head's popping out,' I said. Lying, I thought.

But when the doctor checked, he said, 'Ah yes, good spot. Now we have to push. Don't waste the contractions and it'll be over in five minutes.'

Ten minutes later, no sign of Kiki, so the doctor pulled out something that looked like a plumber's tool and shoved it on the baby's head. 'Have to use suction extraction,' he said. 'Big bloody guy.'

'It better be a girl,' I said for Menaka.

And then, my first-ever sighting of Kiki. I can't say she was beautiful because she looked like an alien, covered in blood, but when she was placed on Menaka's chest, she took straight to her breast.

Menaka smiled, her eyes locked on her baby. 'Now can I have some bloody pain relief?'

We had booked the main suite in the maternity ward so we had a sitting room for our visitors. Mum had arrived straight from the airport and she and Aiya waited patiently for us to feed and bathe Kiki, but of course Uncle Thilak didn't. He was in the room with us, barking orders, telling the nurses to use cloth nappies and not diapers, telling them not to use soap.

The next day, Menaka watched on TV, Kiki to her breast, as news filtered in that the LTTE had said on their website, 'This battle has reached its bitter end... We have decided to silence our guns. Our only regrets are for the lives lost and that we could not hold out for longer.'

Each visitor brought the latest news, each time more elaborate, more ridiculous, but Menaka lapped it up. She had to sit on a foam doughnut because of trauma to her backside, but the news seemed to ease the pain a bit.

'The war ending must mean so much to you all,' my mother said.

'More than anything,' Menaka said, 'it means we can get provisions to the IDPs. To people who need it. I can't wait.'

In the background, Kiki asked for more milk.

At that time, Kiki wouldn't have known, nor probably cared, that she would only get breast milk for ten days – that was how long Menaka was asked to rest. After that, she just couldn't hold herself back. She went to the north for a day but came back after a week.

So, from the age of ten days, I became Kiki's chief caregiver and fed her exclusively with formula. In my head I justified this by thinking that, one day, Kiki would be so proud of her mother knowing how she sacrificed everything to help the people of her country.

The parties on the streets lasted for a while, yet, not everyone joined in. While we were all relieved that there would be no more bombs, we were sensitive to those thousands who had died or lost loved ones.

We didn't know it back then, but the war, or the end of it, had taken Menaka away from us.

thirteen

Menaka is coming home to spend just her sixth night here in the two weeks since we moved in.

The new house is open, breezy and with a lot of glass and natural light. The standout feature is the blue roof which slopes down into the paddy fields. Its finishes are to Menaka's specifications. I may have done it differently – less shoe space, for example – so it's annoying that she's not more enthusiastic about us moving in.

She's late again, and comes to our bedroom, bouncing, high-pitched talking.

'I have it,' she says. 'I have *Killing Fields* on this pen-drive.'

Killing Fields is a documentary that has been creating great anguish here since it was aired on Channel Four last night. It accuses the government of serious human rights violations, but Uncle Thilak has already labelled it trash. He says all the footage is faked by Tamil Tigers themselves.

I am not as passionate about this, one way or the other, as Uncle Thilak and Menaka are. Menaka is bound to have a more balanced view than her father, but for now I am much more concerned about the fact that she hasn't even looked in on Kiki. I tell her this and she lies. She tells me she checked on her, but I would have heard it on the baby monitor if she had.

I doze off during Menaka's screening of the documentary. Maybe it's lazy to say it wasn't my war, but it wasn't. I'd rather this criticism hadn't come out of England, because it could provoke a backlash against us here. But I doubt it.

I wake to Menaka on the phone with Gayan. Speaking fast, speaking loud, barely pausing for breath.

I can't make out whether she is critical of Channel Four or not. I think she's excited that the coverage may help her fund-raising for IDP camps.

Her energy overflows into bed. She's on top of me. I barely move. I feel like a piece of meat. Never thought I would be upset saying that.

I'm not.

In the morning she makes Kiki pancakes.

Kiki can now say lots of words. Daddy, Seeya, yes, no, Kiki, Dora, giraffe... But she can't say Mama.

I don't think she really knows who Menaka is.

As grateful as I am that my wife will be home all day, I wonder if it is safe for both Uncle Thilak and me to go into town. We are the only familiar faces to Kiki. Aiya used to be, but he's in Australia now, married to a sari-wearing Kandyan with an unused PhD.

But Uncle Thilak insists. We have to sign Kiki up at my old school. Pay the advance. Check out their controls for dengue mosquitoes.

All through the journey he blames me for *Killing Fields*. I try to tell him I haven't even seen it, but he asks me again and again to say something.

'Why you bastards siding with the Tigers? They bombed our banks and our children.'

I try to argue that maybe there are two sides to everything but he slaps down whatever I say.

'The West is still out to destroy us,' he says. '*Suddha* bastards out to cut us off. White buggers know the future is brown and yellow and they can't handle it. Pandering to the bloody Tigers shouting in the UK.'

'What colour are the Tigers?'

'Typical Brit smart arse. Tell me, your country labelled Tigers a terrorist organisation, no?'

'So you keep telling me.'

'Like Al Qaeda?'

I ignore him.

'But in England,' he says, 'you allow Tiger supporters to march with LTTE flags. But not Al Qaeda?'

I remain silent because I am naive about all of this. When I used to socialise, pre-Kiki, my friends would talk about such things, but now I am in a baby bubble and I have no argument about this because I have no knowledge.

We approach the British High Commission on Buller's Road, but we can't pass. A crowd, a few thousand strong, brandish professionally printed banners and posters.

Too orchestrated.

Government ministers preach into megaphones. A Buddhist monk too.

Others bang on the gate of the High Commission and hurl stones at its glass roof.

Uncle Thilak says, 'This is a bloody embarrassment. BBC cameras here also.' He points at a group of men, red-eyed, shirtless, dancing *baila*. Stumbling.

'Loku Master has sent buses to the villages. Sent arrack and rice packets. Told these buggers to get on the buses and come here to protest something they have no idea about.'

'Who's Loku Master?' I ask.

'Some minor bloody minister trying to win favour with the

big wigs. Bloody idiots. There are enough and more people like me – lawyers, doctors, professionals – who would come to protest with signs which make sense. Look at those.'

The signs he points to say:

'Channel Four, you are a Whore.'

'We're not your land, England.'

Uncle Thilak shakes his head. 'So bloody embarrassing. They'll show this in the UK.'

I survey the lay of the road to see if I can U-turn, but there's simply no way out. 'Why do you care if they show it in England? Surely it doesn't matter to you what a bunch of whites think of your country.'

'Do you have a cap in here?' he asks. 'Cover your bloody blonde hair.'

I know why he wants me to do this. There is a group of stumbling men in sarongs, the fire of hell in their bloodshot eyes, carrying iron bars and bicycle chains, heading towards us.

I don't have a cap, so I cover my head with one of Kiki's shawls.

It's too late. They hit my window with their palms. Their sweat trickles down the glass. They laugh. Say something. Chant something.

'The white man is not so cocky now,' Uncle Thilak says. 'That's what they're chanting. It's not looking good. Drive.'

There is nowhere to go. I would have no qualms about driving over them to save myself but we're jammed in between cars. I beep the horn as often as I can. Wave to a policeman, but he turns away from me.

'Look after Kiki, please,' I text my wife.

One man, his face scarred from the top of his moustache to the base of his right eye, slams an iron bar against the windscreen and a spider-web crack forms.

Uncle Thilak opens his door and we're overwhelmed by body odour and noise. He is helped out by the people on his side.

'The *suddha* treating you like a slave?' someone asks.

'No, no, no. He's my friend. The *suddha* is my friend. He's on our side.'

The mob slaps him back and forth. Punches. The wound on his neck opens up.

I lean over into the passenger seat and try to pull him back into the car but someone whips bicycle chains across my arms.

They pull me out and pass me over their heads like a rock star at a concert. I can see the clouds; they are low enough to open up soon, and maybe wash this scum away.

I'm on the pavement, slippered feet kicking me in my ribs, a man squatting on my chest pummelling me with a bloody fist.

I picture Kiki and I cry. I cry and plead. 'I have a baby.'

'He's one of us,' Uncle Thilak says. 'Get off him.'

He is next to me on the pavement. They punch and kick him. I'm not sure he can take this.

'He's an old man,' I shout. 'You'll kill him.' But I can't breathe. Too many bodies on me now. Their sweat drips into my mouth. My eyes are swollen shut. I am howling.

'Uncle Thilak?'

There is no answer.

Whistles. Whistles and belts being swung like whips.

The sounds of walkie talkies. The buzz of sirens.

Thunder and the drumming of rain, scattering those around us.

'I'll get a head-cold,' a thug says.

'Amma told me not to stay in the rain,' says another.

Silence but for the rain. Rain in my mouth, up my nose.

Someone props me up. I force one eye open.

Policemen with batons and belts chase the thugs.

A cop holds an umbrella above me, apologises. Says this isn't what his country is about.

There is no sign of Uncle Thilak. I ask where he is.

No one knows.

fourteen

The cop escorts me in an ambulance to General Hospital. He strokes my arm all the way there. Says sorry a thousand times. Says he will make sure the people responsible pay for it. Tells me this is the fault of one man. One man who arranged this thuggery. Got poor people drunk. Told them they'd be rich if they thrashed some white men.

Sorry, sorry, sorry. This is not what we're about, he says.

I try to open my eyes, but can't. My phone is smashed so I give the cop the number and ask him to call my wife.

Kiki is fine. Menaka will bring her. She asks about her father, but I have no idea where he is and neither does the cop. I suggest she keep trying his number.

I wake up in a dormitory with about thirty other men, each sweating more than the other. The fan above me is moving at the speed I blink and all the windows are open to the dust and bus horns of the street outside.

I feel okay. Good, in fact. I must be on something, morphine maybe. My eyes can open enough to see.

The man in the bed next to me has a fake leg resting against a chair.

Makes me check. I have two legs. I can just about feel them.

I try to lift my left arm to scratch my nose, but I can't. My right arm is okay though. I jerk myself up when I hear Kiki crying. She's in Menaka's arms, trying to get out. Menaka slides across the mopped floors, rushing to get to me.

'Sorry I took so long,' Menaka says.

I point at Kiki. 'Have you put mosquito lotion on her?'

'I was in such a rush.'

'Put some on please, baba.'

'I didn't bring any.'

I try to get out of bed to take Kiki home myself but can't. Two people I know have lost kids to dengue. If Kiki ever got it, I'd die.

'Take her home, please.'

'Babe, it's okay. We're only out for an hour or two.'

I grunt. And again. 'You think mosquitoes are going to say, don't bite that child because she's only out for an hour or two?'

Kiki is crying and leaning out of Menaka's arms, trying to get to me. I stroke her face and make some noises which interest her, but possibly not as much as they interest the other patients. It feels like everyone is watching me.

I wrap Kiki in my sheet to protect her from mosquitoes but she tries to get herself onto the floor.

'They found Thathi,' Menaka says. 'Took him to ICU.'

I tip someone to push me in a wheelchair with a squirming Kiki on my lap. I hold her down with my one functioning arm, but each time she moves, my ribs crackle.

Menaka jogs ahead of us, calling for her father.

She throws her hands to her head when she finds his room.

He looks bad.

He has less teeth than before. Less hair even. His eyes are

sealed shut, he has pornstar lips now. And he's attached to machines I could not possibly describe.

'It was that white husband of yours,' he says. 'His fault.'

꙳

I manage to persuade the doctors to release me into the care of a private hospital. I get a suite so Menaka and Kiki are able to move in with me. Menaka appears to be more relieved than me, having complained that Kiki did nothing but cry all night.

But now that she is back with me, Kiki is all smiles, except when I refuse to carry her. That's the main restriction imposed on me by the doctors.

Uncle Thilak is choppered over to the ICU in the same hospital, so Menaka has an excuse to get away from Kiki even though I know that she will only be allowed into ICU twice a day. She returns to us eventually and I feel sorry for her. She looks drained, destroyed even. None of the same bounce she displays when being interviewed on TV.

'Thathi's awake,' she says. 'Out of imminent danger.'

My breathing eases and my pain subsides a touch, but I guess either of these things could be the work of morphine. Still, there's no looking past it. The old bastard, the man who tried to get me deported, the man who didn't want me to marry his daughter...this man, maybe saved my life. Put his own life on the line for me.

'Can I go see him?'

'He demands that I not allow you anywhere near him,' Menaka says. 'But he did ask how you were.'

Kiki starts howling when Menaka looks at her.

'That child really doesn't like me, does she? Daddy's girl.'

'How long will your father have to be in ICU?'

'He'll be out tomorrow, but the doctor in-charge found something in his mouth. Could be a tumour.'

⋇◠⋇

Three days later, I have brought Kiki to see Uncle Thilak. I send her in ahead of me to surprise him, but I am the one surprised as there is no acknowledgement of her presence. I stick my head round the corner. Menaka is on the sofa, crying, head in hands. A doctor is sitting at the desk. Uncle Thilak looks blank in bed.

'Bad news?' I ask.

'Afraid so,' the doctor says.

'They want me to have more radiotherapy, but no way,' Uncle Thilak says.

I shuffle towards him, while Kiki tries to jump for everyone's entertainment.

'Is there an alternative to it?' I ask.

'There sure is,' the doctor says, making Menaka look up. 'Death.'

'Nothing else?' I ask.

'Nothing. Even with radiotherapy and chemo, it's unlikely he'll beat this one.'

'How long, doctor?' Uncle Thilak asks.

'A year, two at tops.' The doctor stands by Menaka. 'I did tell you, you had to bring him for check-ups. I can't believe you allowed him to drink and smoke.'

I grab the doctor's arm. 'Not the time, please.'

'It's important that you look after him this time. Make his last couple of years more comfortable.'

'Last couple of years?' Uncle Thilak props himself up. 'So you're quitting on me?'

'You quit on yourself, sir, when you chose not to give up smoking.'

Menaka cries real tears. Very different to how I've seen her cry before. It makes me fall in love with her again. Maybe she still has a functioning heart.

It looks like Uncle Thilak doesn't. He shows no emotion. His face is almost featureless, until I hand Kiki to him and she says, 'Seeya.' She laughs. She smiles. She whacks her fists against his shoulders in joy.

Uncle Thilak has tears rolling down his face.

So do I.

fifteen

I sometimes ask myself, how will Uncle Thilak's death affect me?

I had a nanny once, who fed Kiki hot milk and burnt her tongue. Another dressed her up as a boy and took pictures, make-believe for the son she never had. It freaked me out.

So, yeah, in practical terms, the loss of the one caregiver I trust other than myself is big.

Aiya's good with Kiki but he's in Sydney most of the year, and Menaka can no longer give a shit if Kiki's tongue's burnt or she's dressed as a ladyboy.

It wasn't always like this. The first few months of Kiki's life, Menaka used to annoy me by emailing me from wherever she was on the island, with instructions as to how I should look after Kiki. I think she got the instructions from a WhatsApp thread she shared with parents who spent all their time with their babies.

Much like me.

Back then, she worried about Kiki. Maybe I should be flattered now. Maybe she trusts me to do a good job on my own.

But, have I done this all on my own? Not really. Uncle Thilak has filled the void left by Menaka and that will be my biggest loss when he 'expires', as they say here.

That, and my source of funding. He pays for everything. I have no income, no visa that allows me to earn an income. I'm a single father in everything but the law.

I know the old man will leave Kiki enough money for us. It's not something I worry about.

But do I lose a friend? I don't know the answer. He treats me like shit, abuses me, picks on my faults, defies me, mocks me.

My colour disgusts him and he hates the way I bring up Kiki.

How can he be a friend?

But if he's not one, why did the news of his expected early check-out make me cry?

There's no hiding from the fact that I am a little jealous of him too.

Kiki shows him too much affection, it pisses me off. Kiki laughs at his crap faces and stunts, it pisses me off. The way he wants me to wash her without putting her in bath water. The way he wants me to put her in frilly dresses, pierce her ears. The way he shuns her routines.

Pisses me off.

Kiki backs up against him, gives him a book to read to her, pisses me off.

Sits on his lap. Cuddles him. Strokes his flaky skin. Laughs when he fights her. Laughs when he pretends she is too strong for him. Their battles over Lego towers.

Pisses me off.

I do the hard yards. I do the dirty jobs: nappy changes, feeding, scolding.

She cries when he leaves the house, but not when I do. She never sees his tantrums, his potential violence, the fear he instills.

Do I worry about how sad she'll be when he dies? Yes, of course I do, but in the back of my mind I think, come that day, I won't have to share her affection.

These thoughts eat at my conscience and I tell Uncle Thilak to move in with us. He makes it sound like it's a damn chore for him.

Menaka has to take him for radiotherapy everyday. Maybe after that he'll need more chemo, maybe more surgery. Easier having him at ours than going to pick him up.

He insisted on, and paid for, a guest wing to our house, designed like a mud hut at the bottom of our sloped garden, but it's not practical to use that now. Instead, I put him in a room between us and Kiki. A room I had assumed would be for our next child, but Menaka won't even talk about that possibility.

Menaka takes her nursing duties seriously: packs his bag; straps him in the car; takes him to Maharagama for his radiotherapy. So she can do it. She can care for people.

I respect her again, until she is commissioned to make a documentary for CNN about a charity worker (herself) she has nominated for an award.

I have to send Uncle Thilak with driver Ranjith everyday. That shit ain't right.

Mornings are Kiki and Daddy time. Reading, teaching, feeding and filling in the hours she would normally be at nursery but for the holidays. Afternoons we go on outings and Uncle Thilak comes. Sometimes we swim, sometimes we go to Independence Square and she climbs the stairs to the pillars of Sri Lankan freedom. Or we walk around the lake near Parliament, Kiki chasing after, or running away from, other kids her age.

Today we go to Fun Factory. Ranjith drives us and I sit in the back, in between Kiki in her car-seat and Uncle Thilak on his plastic sheet.

He has accidents, occasionally, so I carry a change bag for him too. Of course he shouts at me for doing this, but I've developed Aiya's Zen ability to switch off when he does so.

I bump into Samantha, a yummy mummy I know from Jitterbugs classes, with a gorgeous mixed-race daughter called Tara. While I speak to her, Kiki in my arms, Uncle Thilak flaps his hands around, clapping like a mad man, running in circles, cursing.

'Come on, you little bastard,' he says.

I fake a laugh. 'He's trying to kill a mosquito.'

Samantha nods and Tara copies her. As if to say, thanks. You're helping us all. 'Dengue's so scary,' she says. 'A guy I used to work with lost a child to it.' She says something else too, but I miss it because I am chasing around this bloody mosquito.

'Fast bugger,' Uncle Thilak says. 'Get out of the way, *suddha*, get out the way.'

'He's there,' I say. 'On Jumbo's ears.'

Uncle Thilak takes a huge swipe at the stuffed elephant Tara is holding, knocking it out of her hands. 'Ah, got him.'

'Guys, come on,' Samantha says. She kneels down to hug her daughter, who appears to be too shocked to cry.

Uncle Thilak shows me his hand. The mosquito is squashed in blood, meaning it must have had a few bites of people. I use my fingers to pick the mosquito up by the legs. 'They're black,' I say.

'Thank God,' Uncle Thilak says.

Samantha, having chased after Kiki for me, now has her in her arms. 'What does that mean?'

'Mosquitoes that can carry dengue have striped legs.'

'Oh, wow,' Samantha says. 'Didn't know that.'

'God, becoming parents makes us boring, no?' I say.

'Were you ever interesting?' Uncle Thilak asks.

I follow Kiki around the ball-pit, the trampoline and the slides. Uncle Thilak helps her dress up as a doctor and takes her up to the reading level to flick through books.

I have to admire him. He moans like hell when Kiki is not around; he shouts, screams, acts like a little brat, but in her company, he's the teacher's pet. You wouldn't know he was in any discomfort. If Kiki remembers him after he dies, she'll tell everyone he was a man who was never in a bad mood.

Uncle Thilak falls asleep on the beanbag in the reading area and Kiki tries to climb down the stairs on her own. I spot her before she falls.

She points behind me. 'Look, a shepherd costume.'

I turn and my eyes lock on an Arab father in full headgear. So not a shepherd costume! Oh dear.

Kiki starts chasing after a group of six-year-olds in the care of the Arab/shepherd. She follows them to the trampoline, then bounces with them until they notice her and leave. They dive into the ball-pit and Kiki leaps in after them.

'There's that little girl...*again*,' one of them says.

Six-year-olds clearly don't like being followed by two-year-olds.

I should have intervened, but Kiki has already shadowed them to the dressing-up booth. She puts on a hat that should have completed one of mean girls' outfits. Not a good idea. Head mean girl pushes her to the floor.

'Stop following us.'

They leap up the steps to the slides. Kiki's gaze is locked on them, her eyes as blank as Uncle Thilak's after his beating.

I hold my breath and rub my eyes, squatting next to her, stroking her hair. She doesn't cry, but neither does she acknowledge me.

Uncle Thilak is now on the other side of her, fury in his eyes.

Patting her back. 'Those girls are evil bitches,' he says. His choice of vocabulary is questionable, but it's pretty much what I wanted to say. He lifts Kiki up and winces. She's on his shoulders, putting blocks onto a tower the mean girls made. They couldn't get it higher than it is but now Kiki can.

Uncle Thilak leans over to me and cups his hand round my ear. 'Need the change bag.'

'Okay,' I say. 'I'll take her.'

He snarls. Literally bares his teeth. Lifts her onto my shoulders. 'Not hers. Mine.'

I hand him his change bag. It's stocked with disposable underwear, wipes and a plastic bag for soiled pants.

I carry Kiki up the stairs to read to her. She finds clumps of Uncle Thilak's hair on the beanbag and tries to put them in her mouth, shaking her legs out when I try to stop her.

From below, Uncle Thilak says, 'Ice cream. Kiki, my darling, all the damn ice cream in the world.' He stares at the mean girls. 'Good children get lots of ice cream.'

I carry Kiki to the car. Uncle Thilak says he'll be a minute or two. I assume he has to go to the bathroom again.

Kiki devours a packet of Tiny Teddies. I tap the steering wheel wondering why the old man is taking so long.

The door to Fun Factory opens. Uncle Thilak is following the Arab out, wagging his finger at him because he is the head mean girl's father. The Arab picks up his daughter and shuffles away as fast as he can. Uncle Thilak sends him off with some interesting hand gestures before getting into the car, slapping his hands together, proud that he stood up for Kiki. Something I would have liked to do if I had the balls.

sixteen

Menaka must be reading some female empowerment shit and a book of break-up clichés.

First, she tells me we need to talk. Doesn't it always start like that? Then she tells me we have to work things out. Decide what we both want.

So I think about it. I am ready to fight for her because when I agreed to marry her, I knew I'd have to make compromises. I think back to what the astrologer said. What I laughed at. He told us things would not always be easy and we'd have to be understanding of each other's strengths and weaknesses. By getting married, we were signing up to these challenges.

But she was giving up far too easily.

I have two more weeks to figure out what to say to her before she returns from the north. Her suggestion. Wait till she comes back to thrash things out.

On the way for a swim with Kiki, at Water's Edge, I pull over when I get a series of text messages from Menaka. It's one week before my deadline.

'I'm in Jaffna and will be here for the rest of the month. This is very difficult to say, so I'm just going to get straight to it.

'I am not sure if we are right for each other. We're too different. I'm very ambitious and I want to make a difference to the world. I feel like you're holding me back.

'I still love you, but I don't think I'm in love with you.

'I want to explore the world and it seems you're too content with what you have. You're happy to sit around and watch the world go by, whereas I want to be the one moving it.

'I guess I knew who you were. So it's not you, it's me. I need to sort my life out. I need space and time alone. Time away from a relationship. I need to figure out some things for myself.

'I see you as a father and how much love you have for your daughter and I think, there's no room for me. You have no love left to give me.

'Maybe you want a stay-at-home wife. I could never be that. I can't give you what you need.

'You deserve better. I think we're meant to be just friends and you'll make someone very happy one day.

'Please don't reply. I need time to clear my head.'

The signs have been there, but maybe in my preoccupation with Kiki, I didn't see them. Maybe I never thought this could happen while Uncle Thilak's dying; while I am caring for him in her place.

I drive the car onto the pavement. Kiki is agitated that we are not moving and starts to whine and kick the back of the passenger seat.

I reply before thinking about it:

'Baba, I think we need to talk. I've been neglecting you because of Kiki and your father so my head's not been straight. I guess we don't do anything romantic anymore. We never go on dates or buy each other presents and that's all my fault. I know you'll give me another chance to show you how much I love you. How much I need to be with you and how much I want to spend my whole life with you.'

I don't mention how odd I think it is that Menaka refers to Kiki as *my* daughter. Not *our* daughter.

I send the message and then think, you know what, this is my bloody wife. I should be speaking to her on the phone. A beggar taps on the passenger window with the stump of his arm and, on my side, a cop tells me off for parking on the pavement. Costs me a five-hundred-rupee bribe but he tells me to come again.

I drive and dial Menaka.

She doesn't answer until the fourth call.

'Yes,' she says.

'Kiki's in the back and you're on speakerphone,' I say.

'You got my texts?'

'Yes, and I replied. Baba, we just need to give ourselves another chance. I know we're right for each other.'

'We barely spend any time together, and you know what? I just don't miss you at all.'

That feels like a kick in the nuts. My chest hurts. I lean towards the air conditioner vents to suck in air. Putting the speaker off, I lift the phone to my ear.

'Do you miss me?' she asks. 'Honestly?'

'Of course I do.' I'm not sure I mean it. 'But I don't have a choice. I haven't wanted to tie you down. You know, other men would try to tie –'

'Well that's the thing. Maybe other men would have more passion than you. More pride.'

'We need you,' I say.

'It's over. I mean, I know it's over. There's no going back. It would all be fake.'

'One more chance, please.'

She doesn't say anything for what seems like an hour before mumbling something I must have misheard. I ask her to repeat herself.

'There's someone else I'm interested in,' she says.

I'm silent. This is the biggest blow you can possibly get. Your wife being more interested in another man than you.

'I mean,' she says, 'we haven't done anything. It's just that he gets me. He knows what I want and what I need. He knows what makes me tick. He understands my ambition. How important my success is.'

Kiki being in the back keeps me calm, even though she's crying intermittently. 'I thought you said you needed some space.'

'Yes, I do. We're not going to do anything till I'm ready.'

I throw my phone to the floor so that I can't hear Menaka's whiny voice anymore.

I try to park and get out to unstrap Kiki but the Water's Edge security guard calls me back and tells me I need to move the car. I try to ask him why but he can't speak English. He directs me back out of my parking spot, then back into it, possibly an inch and a half further to the left than I was before. I roll down my window to shout at him but he smiles and directs me forward. I can see that I am about to hit the wall in front of me but he keeps beckoning me on with a stiff, robotic wave that he must have practised. Again I stop, but he taps the front of the car and calls me forward. Kiki is whining in the back, so I follow instructions until he hammers the bonnet and screams, '*Stop.*'

I get out of the car even though I can see the security guard measuring whether I am exactly in the middle of the two yellow lines. 'No way,' I say. 'I'm not moving.'

The rest of the car park, maybe four hundred parking spaces, is half empty anyway.

I scoop Kiki into my arms even though she wants to walk. 'Cars could come,' I say.

I have to balance her float on my head, like a hat, and I have her bag on one shoulder and mine on the other.

The security guard says something.

'What the hell do you want?' I ask.

Pointing behind me, he bends to pick something up. 'Baby ishoe,' he says. 'Baby ishoe.'

'*Istuti*,' I say. Thank you. One of the few Sinhala words I know.

⁂

We ascend the stairs we need to climb to be able to descend another set of stairs to the pool. As I change Kiki, a seaplane lands on the man-made lake by the clubhouse, scattering birds towards us. I jump straight into the pool, holding my daughter in outstretched arms. I want to clear my mind, but I can't, and I want to get back to my phone. Kiki demands to be thrown in the air, but after the fourth throw I lose patience and tell her we have to get out. She hits me on the shoulders with clenched fists. I shake her. 'Stop, for Christ's sake.'

Everyone – on the phone, the kids taking swimming lessons, the coaches wearing huge hats to stop their burnt faces from getting more burnt, the waiters, the lifeguards, the social climbers, the people from the gym above us – every single person at Water's Edge turns to face me, so I throw Kiki up and down a couple more times, but she's already crying.

'Be quiet,' I say. 'You're embarrassing me.'

'I hate you,' she says.

'Join the bloody club,' I say.

I think most of the Water's Edge membership now wants to join that club too.

I call Uncle Thilak and say I'm about to drop Kiki home in his care. He pretends it's a nuisance, but has the same excitement in his voice he always does when he's about to meet his granddaughter.

When we get home and drive up our stone path, towards the open veranda of my house, Kiki doesn't allow me to kiss her goodbye. She jumps out of the car as soon as I have undone her seatbelt and sprints into Uncle Thilak's brittle arms, knocking him back into his planter's chair.

I drive, maybe two hundred metres, then send these text messages to Menaka:

'You're a selfish bitch. Not once have you mentioned your daughter, or your father, or your husband. It's all me me me me me. And who gives a shit about your pokey little career? You're probably the least successful person I know. What difference have you made? You want to leave your mark on the world? Try acknowledging your daughter's existence.'

Her reply, which came in between much more abuse from me: 'No need to get personal.'

That's it. That's all she says. In between dumping me.

Still no mention of Kiki.

I ask Uncle Thilak if he and the nurse can look after Kiki tonight. He knows what's happening, but he doesn't say he told me so. Aiya is in town with his sari-wearing wife, carrying out Menaka's family duties. He texts me to say he's so sorry. Menaka has always been like this. Single-minded. Never one to settle down and care for kids.

I go out drinking with JoJo and Robin at the Sinhalese Sports Club, sitting in the stadium of the Test match pitch, outside the main bar so that we can smoke.

'You may be better off without her,' Robin says.

'Thinks she's a celebrity,' JoJo says. 'Someone special.'

Robin tops up my drink. 'Always been arrogant.'

'Don't get me wrong,' JoJo says. 'She's a hot bitch and I'd do her if –'

'Please,' I say.

'Too soon?' JoJo asks.

'Always will be,' I say.

'Get you some chicks tonight,' JoJo says. 'Don't tell them you're broken up; chicks love a taken man.'

'Not the time,' Robin says. He puts his palms on my thighs, leans forward. 'She manipulated you like she manipulates everyone. Everything's about her.'

I close my eyes and lean against a plastic bucket seat in front of me. What they say hurts, either because I still love her or because I feel stupid that I let her use me like this.

Robin and JoJo try their best to distract me. Talk of cricket, talk of casinos and jokes and Twitter spoofs. But I don't take much in. All I can think of is Menaka. I love her. More so than before she dumped me. Much more. Even though I didn't see her much, she was mine so that was okay.

Now she's about to be someone else's.

After my eighth arrack I text Menaka:

'I love you so much and so does Kiki. Give us another chance.'

I go to the loo inside the bar but when done, instead of turning back to JoJo and Robin, I walk past the swimming pool and onto the main road, where I flag down a trishaw.

I get calls from the boys, asking where I am but my phone goes dead and I have to get home to charge it in case Menaka wants to call me. To change her mind.

I wake up the next morning not knowing how I got into bed. Not knowing if I looked in on Kiki when I got home. I check my phone to see if Menaka has texted, but I have messages only from Aiya, Jimmy, JoJo, Robin and Mum. I don't bother reading any of them. Instead, I check sent messages. It seems last night I sent seventy-four messages to Menaka. The last ten or twenty are incomprehensible. Just drunken gibberish, which is a relief.

But, oh dear God, the other messages go from saying she is the most beautiful girl in the world to saying she is a fat slut who needs lots of men to feel fulfilled. That her career is a sham and that she is so pretentious, fake and up her own arse.

Kiki finds me on the sofa and seems to have forgotten about me shouting at her. She bounces up and down on my chest. Pleasant for my emotions, not so much for my hangover.

'Can you go find Seeya for me, baba?' I ask.

She's at the age where she loves to please and to show that she can follow instructions so she sets off up the stairs.

'Please don't start anything with the other man,' I text Menaka. 'Give me another chance.'

While Seeya is looking after Kiki, I have a shower and scrub the smell of smoke out of my hair. I brush my teeth three times to get the stench of arrack out of my mouth but it doesn't work. Neither does mouthwash. Even my crap reeks of arrack and it's blue, suggesting that at some stage the night before I must have stopped off at the Union Bar for a blue margarita, but who the hell with?

I get a call from my network provider saying Menaka has reported me for sending her abusive texts. I tell them she is my wife and she's with another man and they appear to side with me, but still say they have had to block me from calling or texting her number, even though her number is under my name and I pay the bill (with Uncle Thilak's money).

I look for Gayan to find out where Menaka is, but he is out of town on work too.

Uncle Thilak gets Leg-breaker Gunesekera to help me find Menaka's address in Jaffna. 'I know my daughter,' he says. 'She doesn't leave one branch until she is already holding another.'

'I've got to try,' I say.

'Understood,' he says. 'But I warned you, okay?'

'I'll be gone just one night.'

He says, 'You wouldn't even leave Kiki for two hours before. Don't let this become a slippery slope like it did for me when I was your age.'

I'm an hour outside Colombo when I remember that I didn't even kiss Kiki goodbye.

Armed with eighty-eight red roses, a banoffee pie in a cool box and a one-hundred-thousand rupee pair of diamond earrings, I Google-map my way up to Jaffna. I want to surprise her. I want to win her back before she falls into the arms of the other man. In my head I am picturing a white man, because she has always had a thing for them; for us, I mean. I plot, in my mind, how I can ask Uncle Thilak to get him deported. For Kiki's sake. I know he'll do it for Kiki's sake. I think about how my Sri Lankan friends will stand up for me; as their *suddha*. Their white man. This other bastard doesn't have a chance.

I find the bungalow she is staying in. It is small, but impeccably clean and newly painted, white, with a blue roof like the one she chose for the house we built together.

I ring the bell.

Gayan answers.

It clicks. How can I be surprised?

Second cousins. The forbidden love that Menaka yearns for.

Eventually, she comes to the door.

'Is it him?' I ask.

She nods and mouths, 'I'm sorry.'

seventeen

Uncle Thilak is preparing for the first operation of his second cancer. I am with him for a couple of hours at the hospital while Aiya and his sari-wearing wife take Kiki to the zoo. The doctor comes in to brief us, and from the sound of things, part of Uncle Thilak's tongue is about to be removed. If this bothers him, he doesn't show it. His greater concern seems to be when he will be allowed to drink and smoke again post-operation.

Menaka and Aiya are going to be at the hospital when he is taken into surgery so I have to get out soon. I'm not ready to see my wife with Gayan and that stupid zig-zag beard. Holding hands. Kissing, sharing their common DNA. No one's ready for that creepy shit. Uncle Thilak denies it's happening. 'Dying is less painful than accepting that,' he says.

Aiya texts me throughout the operation, pretty much to say they have no idea what's going on as no news is coming out of the theatre. Kiki is asleep so I am able to sit on my bedroom balcony overlooking the paddy fields, drinking the beer, and smoking the cigarette Uncle Thilak is likely dreaming about.

'He's out,' Aiya messages. 'In good spirits, but he's asking to see Kiki.'

'Will Menaka be there?'

'Likely, yes, but if you don't want to see her, I can come down and get Kiki from your car.'

I must oblige. If it was me in hospital, the one thing that could cheer me up would be Kiki.

Kiki has been with Uncle Thilak for just over an hour, but it seems like much longer because I know Gayan is up there as well. I can't stand the thought of him trying to carry her, styling her hair. Worse, what if Kiki's laughing at his jokes, climbing all over him, asking to be thrown in the air?

That's my gig.

It's been an hour and a half when I see Aiya walking my little girl back to the car. She buries her face in my shoulder, hugs me, taps my back in a rather patronising sorry-you-couldn't-come-up manner.

'Uncle Gayan wanted Seeya to move in with them, but he said no.'

I feel warm and fuzzy inside. 'He's coming back to us?'

'Yes, Daddy. I don't think he likes Uncle Gayan. I don't like Uncle Gayan.'

So Uncle Thilak chose us ahead of living with his own daughter. He sees through Gayan's shit. Realises he's just after his money.

Money I would be a bit screwed without.

Aiya straps Kiki in and taps me on the back. 'Hope you're okay, *machang*.' He walks away, turns and knocks on my window. 'I must say I respect you. Can only guess what you must be going through, but you're being strong for your daughter. If it makes you feel any better, my sari-wearing wife sides with you on this.' He leans past me and says to Kiki, 'Don't forget to give him the note from Seeya.'

'What note?' I am excited by this, perhaps more than I should be.

The note says: '*Suddha*, these bloody pussies won't give me what I want. Can you leave Kiki with Aiya this evening and come to visit me with a bottle of Scotch and some Gold Leaf? But *suddha*, these nurse women are on to me so bring the booze in an old Dettol bottle. Or just say it's a urine sample.'

I smile. I know I shouldn't be doing this. He's only bonding with me because he couldn't convince anyone else to break the rules for him, but still. I have missed drinking with the old bugger.

❧

Kiki is excited about being left with Aiya for the evening and asks if she can wear a sari. Menaka had given her a couple of ready-made saris which she could just zip on, but it was so long ago that they are likely to be too small now.

Uncle Thilak calls me four times after 6 p.m., the time he allows himself to start drinking whisky.

When I get to the hospital, I wait a few minutes for the lift because it stops at every floor on the way down to me. By the time it arrives, too many people want to get in and I am scared of catching their germs and taking them home to Kiki.

So I use the stairs. For nine floors.

I'm panting when I get to the nurse's reception and when I ask where his room is, the head nurse, a plump woman with a plump nose and a wide frown, points to the left and then down to my bag.

'What's in that?'

'Urine sample,' I say.

'You're not smuggling alcohol in for the old man, are you?'

'He's just had an operation,' I say. 'No, of course not.'

'Prove it,' she says.

'How can I do that, miss?'

'Drink from the bottle.'

I think she may have got this wrong in her head. 'Why would I drink urine?'

'You wouldn't, so if you did drink, then I am know it is alcohol.'

'Good point.' No idea what she was on about. 'His room?'

'941. But he is in very cranky mood since six o'clock. Very agitated.'

'Okay, don't worry,' I say. 'He's always like that.'

She points me in the direction of the room again. 'And, sir, why are you bring his urine sample from home when he is here?'

I had wondered how I would get round that one. All I can manage is a smile and a wink. The nurse winks back at me.

Uncle Thilak bounces upright in his bed when he sees me enter the room. 'Quick, you bugger, quick.'

'Glasses?' I ask.

'No need, no bloody time.' He drinks the Scotch straight out of the Dettol bottle and smiles, even more crookedly than before. His teeth are rusty brown and point in different directions. He grimaces. Whisky has got to hurt the mouth when you've just had surgery in there.

After he gestures for me to help him out of bed, I push his drip stand along with him as he hobbles into the bathroom. 'Come,' he says.

Oh dear.

'Bring the Gold Leaf.'

'I really don't think it's a good idea to smoke, uncle.'

'*Suddha*, don't worry. The doctor said I had to wait just twenty-four hours after surgery.'

'Did he really?' I ask.

'Yes, maybe.'

'It can't be right.' I look at my watch. 'Anyway, it's only been about four –'

'Bugger also told me that road pollution is much worse than smoking. The exhausts of our buses. Black bloody smoke. The doctor told me standing behind a bus is like smoking two hundred cigarettes.'

'It's probably cheaper, though,' I say.

Uncle Thilak smiles, possibly in recognition of my joke, but more likely because I open the packet of Gold Leaf.

This takes me back to boarding school. Blowing smoke straight into the bathroom exhaust. It's like I'm a fourteen-year-old, sharing a cigarette with the headmaster. But I'm no longer scared of the headmaster; no longer scared of Uncle Thilak.

He puts his arms over my shoulder and I help him back into bed. His Scotch is almost finished but his red eyes light up when he sees me pull out another Dettol bottle.

'*Suddha*, I have something to speak to you about. Won't be easy for me, because I don't trust you.' He tries to smile but can't yet. 'I have to be true to myself. I may not live till a hundred like I had planned and I wonder if you can bring up Kiki without me.

'You may feel my daughter let you down,' he says, 'but I would disagree. If you knew her better than you did when you asked her to marry you, you would have known this was her.'

'Just a second.' I hold up my hand. 'You don't know that she proposed to me?'

'What bloody cock.'

'I promise,' I say. 'She told me not to tell you that, but well, I guess now...'

'Technicality.' He knocked back the rest of the whisky. 'Gayan won't last long. That's the only reason I haven't had him locked up. She's like this. She tries to confront her fear of commitment by committing more, but it just ends up scaring her away from anyone who loves her.'

'Is that really an excuse?' I ask. 'She's never acknowledged her daughter.'

'You never met her mother, but she was exactly the same. On the surface. She loved her children, no doubt about it, but she was too anxious to care for them. Too scared they would rely on her. That boxed her in, made her feel claustrophobic. When Aiya was born, I did all the bathing, feeding, changing. My wife couldn't produce her own milk because it stressed her out. After Menaka was born, she hung around for about a year. When she finally left, she didn't even say goodbye to her daughter. I don't think Menaka can ever forgive her for that, even though she has no idea why she left. She's not interested. Doesn't even acknowledge that she exists.'

'I wanted to ask,' I say, 'why there are no pictures of Menaka's mother anywhere. No sign she even –'

'Is this your story or mine? If it's yours, I'll need more pain relief.'

'It's yours,' I say. 'Your wife left and –'

'– by then I was too caught up in my own career to spend any time with Menaka and she was brought up by nannies. Brace yourself for this. Take a shot of whisky, because it's not easy for me to say these things. To be honest, I'd rather wait till the day I die to open my heart to anyone, let alone you, but I don't know when that day will be. The thing is Menaka...'

Uncle Thilak looks at the ceiling, watches the fan's blades rotate above him and closes his eyes.

I assume he's thinking what to say next. I wait a couple of minutes before I call out his name. He's asleep. The amount of drugs he's on must have knocked him out. He snores like a diesel-powered generator, little pockets of air bubbling under the bandage on his cheek.

I'm tempted to kick the base of his bed to wake him up. Like I did so by accident. I have to know what he wanted to tell me.

Instead, I worry that giving him booze with his drugs could kill him. So I message Aiya asking if he can look after Kiki overnight so that I can monitor his father.

I wake before Uncle Thilak and check whether he has a pulse.

'Why the hell are you holding my hand, *suddha*?' he asks.

I fix him up with a cup of lukewarm tea and he sips, grimaces, and gives me a dirty look. 'Hurts to drink anything –'

'Except whisky,' I say. 'Last night, we were talking and I think you wanted to get something off your chest.'

'You think I'm here for a bloody breast reduction?' He presses a button for the nurse and then lifts a newspaper which then acts as a barrier between us.

It's odd. I find comfort in Uncle Thilak being distant and rude to me again. I want him to be himself. What's the point of fighting to live if you have to be someone else?

⁂

Back home, Uncle Thilak is upstairs in bed. He can't handle as much booze as he used to and his drugs make him drowsy. The only thing I can do is have a drink with JoJo on the veranda of the house I built to share with my wife. The house that she still hasn't contested. Now that Uncle Thilak is back with us, she's off being pretentious somewhere else on the island.

I tell JoJo that whenever I see her on the BBC saying how it is her life's mission to save children in the north, I want to text in, I want to tweet, I want to shout out to the whole world that the bitch doesn't even like her own child. She's so incredibly fake.

JoJo claps. 'Finally, you bugger, you're venting. Not defending her. Bloody fisherman's whore that woman.'

I ask him what he means by the last sentence but he grunts and puts a plate of crab in front of me. 'Eat, eat, you bugger.'

I eat and eat. But I also tell JoJo about the secret Uncle Thilak is not sharing with me.

'Get that bugger's son to tell you. What's the bugger's name?'

'Aiya.'

JoJo slaps his forehead with his open palm. 'No, you bugger, Aiya means older brother. What's the bugger's name? Oh, never mind. Get the bugger hammered and ask him. Tell the bugger to come now. Can put a shot with us.'

I make the call and, once the alcohol has drilled holes into Aiya's defences, he can't stop speaking.

'Thathi kicked Menaka out of the house.' Aiya takes off his glasses and wipes the steel rims. 'When she was fifteen, she had a Tamil boyfriend.'

'Aiyo, *sin*, no?' JoJo says. 'Father kicked her out?'

'Shoved her in a hostel for a year and a half. Said she'd disgraced him. Disgraced the family. Took her out of school in shame. Never visited her. I was the only person from her home life that she had a chance to converse with. Toughened her up. Made her who she is, that hostel.'

'But Uncle Thilak took her back, obviously?' I ask.

'Yes, and he's been trying to make amends ever since. That's why she gets her own way now. Only person who does so with my father.'

JoJo grunts, his eyes closing as he kicks his legs out, knocking over a bottle of arrack.

'Thathi is incapable of criticising her now,' Aiya says. 'Even if she's in the wrong. He won't argue with her, or deny her anything. I know my sister. She's got a good heart but, because of what happened to her before, she thinks Thathi owes her the world.'

'So what does that mean?'

'Either find another house and source of income for Kiki, or get yourself a lawyer. She'll come gunning for everything Thathi has.'

eighteen

My barber in Battaramulla is called Joseph Stalin, and he is also a qualified circumciser and sari-draper. He charges me the equivalent of one-pound-fifty for a haircut and an hour-long head massage. The machine for the massage looks like it has touched a million greasy heads over the last forty years, but it feels great. I can now move my neck without it creaking.

Kiki is at the nursery and I have half an hour until Uncle Thilak is due at the physio.

'Not leaving till those buggers mow the lawn,' he says.

'This is my house, so don't worry about it.'

'Your bloody car is filthy.'

'Just get in or we'll be late.'

'I didn't ask you to take me, *suddha*. Get that straight, okay. I don't want to go for bloody physio.'

'So you're doing me a favour, are you?'

He holds my wrist and pulls himself into the back of my car. 'You love me, I know, but I can't spend every minute of the day with you.' I can feel his breath on my back as I drive. He's leaning over, examining something on my neck. 'You know you have a big cut there?'

I take a hand off the wheel and rub a finger over the cut. 'Jesus, the barber.' It's a gash from his razor, and I try to remember if I saw him inserting a new blade into it.

'Haircut?' he asks. 'Hope you didn't pay for that crap.'

'Nothing wrong with it,' I say.

'You look like a pineapple.'

I touch the back of my neck again. 'Can I get AIDS from the barber?'

'Yes,' Uncle Thilak says. 'If you had unprotected sex with him.'

I look out the window, away from him, so he cannot see me laughing.

༤

Harshi, the physio, works on the scar under Uncle Thilak's chin, promising that she can massage it away. Yeah, bullshit. I sit on a cracked fake-leather sofa next to a pile of magazines from the twentieth century. Above me, a small box TV shows a Sinhala teledrama, volume on full.

Uncle Thilak asks, 'Any more stories about my relatives?'

'I couldn't tell you, I'm afraid.' Harshi pretends to zip her mouth shut. 'But your cousin's wife, Thilini, said something very interesting.'

'Share,' Uncle Thilak says.

'Oh, I couldn't possibly. But basically, she sleeps in a different room to Gehan now.'

'Old news, madam,' Uncle Thilak says. 'Next.'

'There's more,' Harshi says.

'*Suddha*, you should listen to this.'

'I don't get off on gossip,' I grumble.

'White puritan bullshit. Of course you do. You couldn't get off more on gossip if gossip was the name of a little boy at your gay boarding school.'

'I'm not rising to this, Uncle Thilak.'

'How about if I remind you that these are Gayan's parents we're talking about?'

I shake my head and put my earphones on. But of course I want to listen, so I don't play any music on my iPod.

'You never know when you may need this info, *suddha*.' Uncle Thilak buries his face back into the slot on the massage table. 'So Thilini sleeps in a different room, and...?'

'And she gets her...' Harshi looks around, probably more for effect than need, as no one else is there. 'She told me about this ring of cops who sleep with old society ladies for money. And guess what? She's started using them.'

Uncle Thilak spits out laughter. 'That's just too bloody good.'

'She complains about Gehan visiting that karaoke bar. You know, the one with the Chinese, um, prostitutes?'

'The Yellow Pussy?' Uncle Thilak asks.

'That's it, yes.'

My phone rings and it's Jimmy Walsh. I'm reluctant to answer because I find all calls to be intrusive in the age of text messaging. But everyone knows this about me, so they only tend to call in emergency, or if drunk.

It's school time, so there's an even chance Jimmy's not drunk. He tells me the nursery section got in touch with him. Kiki is not well. Nothing to be alarmed about, but she has a temperature of 102 degrees and no energy.

Nothing to worry about? Jesus Jimmy.

Jimmy doesn't know that I've been shitting myself ever since Kiki got bitten by a mosquito eight days ago. I killed the bugger but only after it had bitten her. It had striped legs, confirming that it was the kind that could carry dengue. I stayed up all night googling it and the consensus was that if Kiki contracted dengue, it would show up seven to ten days later.

Like, now.

Jesus Jimmy.

Uncle Thilak insists on coming with me even though I beg him to finish his physio, or I'll have to bring him back later. He doesn't answer, just follows me down the stairs and into the car.

To beat Sri Lankan traffic, sometimes you have to drive Sri Lankan. I put on my hazard lights. I keep one palm flat against the horn. I spend the majority of my time on the wrong side of the road. Uncle Thilak hangs much of his body outside the passenger window, waving people out of the way.

Even the buses slow down for us. That's how Sri Lankan I drive.

The cops don't register that we're doing anything wrong. That's how Sri Lankan I drive.

I park on the pavement. 'Wait here.'

I run through the grounds of this converted rubber estate, past palm trees, kids playing basketball, kids painting, towards the sick room.

'Where is she?' I ask. 'Where is Kiki Trusted?'

Uncle Thilak is behind me. Panting. His face is purple. It sounds like something is blocking his throat. He collapses into a chair, struggling to breath.

Idiot, I think. Idiot, idiot, idiot. 'I told you not to come,' I say. 'No time for you to die right now.'

Kiki's lying face down on a stained plastic sheet in the sick room.

'Kiki, darling.'

No response. All of my worst fears realised. All of them.

I stroke her back. She's breathing. I carry her, so her face is on my shoulder, but she can't lift her head.

I look towards Uncle Thilak. 'Okay?'

He struggles to stand, and taps Kiki's back, tears streaming down his face.

'Uncle, call Dr Farij.' I check my watch. 'I think he's got a clinic at Joseph Fraser now. Tell him to wait there.'

This is Uncle Thilak's strength. He barks the order down the phone.

In the car, Kiki is on Uncle Thilak's lap. Not moving. We drive the car into the nursing home, past a protesting security guard, and park near the lush lawn that leads to where Kiki was born. We storm into Dr Farij's clinic. He's giving a toddler a jab. The toddler screams. Kiki raises her head, looks, then drops it back onto my shoulder.

The doctor is calm. He asks the other parents if they can wait outside for a moment, and tells me to put Kiki on the table. He presses his stethoscope against her chest. Usually, Kiki complains when he does this, because I think she finds it cold. But this time, nothing. Silence.

Her eyes remain closed.

The nurse puts a thermometer under Kiki's arm.

Dr Farij sits behind his desk and takes notes. 'Temperature?' he asks.

'103,' the nurse says.

'Is it dengue?' Uncle Thilak asks.

'We'll see,' Dr Farij says.

Uncle Thilak slams his palm on the desk. 'Tell us the bloody truth, you bugger.'

Calm, quiet, Dr Farij says, 'Give her Calpol to bring the temperature down. Lots of water if you can. Calpol three times a day. Check her tomorrow morning. If she still has a temperature, call me.'

'Come on, doctor, what is it?' Uncle Thilak asks.

I hold his arm, pulling him down into a chair next to me.

The nurse puts Kiki on my lap.

'It's not dengue, no?' I ask.

'Can't rule it out,' the doctor says. 'When did she get the temperature?'

'This morning,' I say.

'Wait three days. If she still has a temperature, we need to do the dengue blood test...'

'Let's just do it now,' Uncle Thilak says.

'Three days. If you did it right now you'd just be traumatising her for nothing. Make her rest.'

'Doctor, I can't see her like this,' I say.

'Try the Calpol. If that works she'll seem normal until it wears off again. Just monitor her.'

The Calpol brings down Kiki's temperature, and although she is still subdued, she does drink her milk and then tries to climb onto the dining table. But as the dose wears off, Kiki falls asleep on my lap. Uncle Thilak and I debate whether we should wake her up to give her more Calpol to get her through the night, but we decide against it.

I try to force Uncle Thilak into bed, but he insists he wants to stay awake in case Kiki needs him. 'Pour me a whisky, *suddha*.'

'Pour it yourself.'

He gives me one of those do-as-I-bloody-tell-you looks so I pour him one.

I gather my pillow and duvet and set myself up on Kiki's floor. I can't bear not sleeping in the same room as her when she's like this. Every few moments, I touch my phone screen to get just enough light to check on her. She's breathing.

I guess it's about one in the morning when I fall asleep.

I wake up, check the time on my phone, which lights up another body on the floor next to me. Uncle Thilak is asleep, his sarong hitched up above his waist, tackle out.

I make sure Kiki is breathing. I cover Uncle Thilak. Check he's breathing.

When I wake up again, my heart goes a little crazy. I see a figure looming directly above me. Looking over my baby. Uncle Thilak.

Kiki's night light is on.

I stand next to Uncle Thilak. He smells of fresh cigarette smoke.

'She's okay?' I ask.

'I think her temperature is almost normal.'

I have to check so I touch the back of my hand to her neck, until she turns her body over. 'She feels hot to me.'

'Let her sleep,' he says. 'Whisky?'

I'm tempted. I check my watch. 'At four in the morning?'

'Why not?' he says. 'You can bring it in here. It's not like we're sleeping much.'

So we have a Scotch. In silence. Much like we normally drink together.

'Dada. Dada. Dada'

I rub my eyes open, see Uncle Thilak, the right side of his face against the terracotta tiles of Kiki's floor, his mouth wide open like a fish, and the two empty glasses by his chin.

'Dada, what are you doing?'

I roll onto my back and look up. Kiki is standing, with her hands on the edge of a cot she is clearly too old for. No, no, no. I'm confused. I'm drunk, maybe.

'She looks good.' Uncle Thilak wakes up. 'Hi, baby girl.'

'Seeya, why you sleeping on my floor?' Kiki has a wide smile on her face.

'I missed you, *chooti kella*.'

She runs on the spot. We have to calm her down because she can't exert herself. I carry her to the living room and put on

Dora the Explorer and get her to lie back on her beanbag in front of the TV.

Uncle Thilak gets the thermometer under her arm.

We wait three minutes. A bloody long time to have to wait.

I grab at the thermometer before Uncle Thilak can; I am not patient enough to wait for him to get his eyes in focus so that he can actually read the damn thing. We stand side by side. I struggle to register exactly where the mercury ends.

Uncle Thilak smiles, because I think he sees me smile.

'It's normal,' I say. 'It's bloody normal.'

Uncle Thilak throws his arms around me, pulls me into his chest, kisses my face. We back-peddle and look at each other, grinning. He pushes me away. 'Bloody gay boy, keep your hands off me.'

'You hugged me,' I say.

'Rubbish, you bugger. You touched my ass like you've wanted to for years.'

He ruffles Kiki's hair and kisses her head, before ambling to the planter's chair on the veranda. He's asleep within twenty seconds.

I pour cans of Red Bull down my throat, but still struggle to keep alert. Kiki stays home, and will do so again tomorrow, so I need to have the energy to look after her without letting her exert herself. I am keen to take her back to the doctor just to be sure she's on the mend. I know he'll say she's fine unless her temperature comes back, but I go anyway. I get a text from Aiya on the way there: 'Thathi told me, and it seems everyone else in his phone book, that you stroked his ass. :-) Glad Kiki's better.'

nineteen

Although I invited Uncle Thilak to stay at our house as a guest, he has taken on the role of lord of the manor. The domestic help won't do anything without his blessing, and I don't blame them because if they do, he curses them in filth. He has the final word on everything. For example, even though he refuses to eat, he chooses our menus and writes our shopping lists.

His body has taken an odd form now. He looks like a plastic bag full of chicken bones. His smile is not just crooked, it is almost as zig-zagged as Gayan's creepy beard. He tells everyone that I am getting fat and he is getting thin because I eat all his food. All he ever wants to eat is fried eggs or cheesecake, and even that I have to force down him. If I left him to it, he'd get all his calories from beer.

I ask him if I am to blame for his hair loss too. His answer is yes, but he always has a different explanation why.

Like, he tells people I slap his head so much, his hair falls out. That's why his head resembles a number eight pool ball, he says: black, smooth and shiny.

He is the one person who knows I wouldn't be here if not for him. I'd be back in the UK, sponging off my parents, even though they don't have much sponge.

I'm not here to care for him. I battled with myself long ago about that. It's not my responsibility. I'm here because he claims he has an injunction stopping me from leaving the country with

Kiki until the divorce and custody battles have played out. I can't begrudge him this. I think he feels he's lost a daughter and all that he really lives for is Kiki.

This doesn't stop me from checking whether I can leave the country, and the reality is that I am legally supposed to fly with a letter of consent from Kiki's mother, and apparently since I am white and Kiki is tanned, I would attract attention at immigration. There's no way around this. I'm told the immigration officials simply don't accept bribes, under any circumstances, unless they are quite big.

And there is the small matter of the divorce. Menaka has not even filed any papers. Eight months after leaving me, she has not served me with anything. Gayan's still on the scene, contrary to Uncle Thilak's predictions. Apparently he bad-mouths me around town at any opportunity. The temptation is there to spread the news that his mother gets sexual favours off cops and that his father is a bona fide card-carrying whore-monger, but that's not my style. Yet.

JoJo suggests I consult a lawyer. If Kiki is left anything substantial in Uncle Thilak's will, I agree, it's just possible that Gayan may encourage Menaka to fight for her custody. Otherwise she wouldn't. Surely. I still don't think she acknowledges Kiki as her child. Today, as with most days, I look at pictures of Kiki when she first came out of Menaka to make sure. Make sure she is the mother.

And that's it. I'd want to kill myself if I ever lost Kiki to anyone, but more so to a mother who shows no love for her. I get cramps just thinking about it. Chest pains. I sweat out the arrack I have made a habit of drinking with Uncle Thilak every night after Kiki goes to bed.

JoJo says I could be accused of trying to speed up Uncle Thilak's death by drinking with him all the time. In fact, he feels so strongly about it that he comes around to put a stop to it, but he ends up doing tequila slammers with Uncle Thilak and they pass out on the same chair.

I wake the nap buddies up and send them to bed. They take turns abusing me.

My eyes open, as usual, at three in the morning. My head pounds less than normal, but I need to drink water. I check on Kiki, nudging her door open, lifting it to stop it from scratching along the floor. I put a hand on her chest to make sure she's breathing. I hold out my hands above her bed to see if it's too cold or too hot with the fan on full.

I walk down the corridor to Uncle Thilak's room.

A smell like ammonia. A smell like arrack. I think he's pissed himself.

I put my hand to his chest to see if he's breathing and lift the sheet over his bare body.

It's the same every night.

Kiki first, then Uncle Thilak.

There's a wet bed two or three times a week.

I meet JoJo at the pool. Even though he's in the water, you can tell he's sweating. I saw him get in, squeeze his head into a cap, and swim two lengths. But best to humour the overweight.

'How many lengths?' I ask.

'Sixty-two.' He stretches his neck. 'Ready for tonight, you bugger? Got some birds coming.'

'Should I be honest? Should I admit I have a daughter who will always come first?'

'Find a bloody bird first, you bugger,' JoJo says.

'But really,' I say, 'what should I do?'

He grunts, ducks his head under water and sets off for another length but stops after three strokes. 'Don't laugh, you bugger. Cramp.'

JoJo arranges dinner at Lagoon. I leave Kiki in the care of Uncle Thilak and Aiya. It's tough saying goodbye to my little beauty. I expect her to howl when I leave but she's shoving me out the door. A sign of her love of Uncle Thilak? Or simply that she wants to prove to me that she's a 'big girl'.

Talking of big girls, the only Sri Lankans on time to dinner at Lagoon are Dilshani and Ishara, and they're huge. I fear for the size of our bill – quality seafood being ordered by girls who starve themselves all day, but give up on their diets once they've had a couple of drinks. This could be dangerous.

Jimmy Walsh lets down the side, a bit, by being a white guy arriving later than the locals. I tap my watch until I notice that he's with a rather cute little blonde girl who he has just recruited to teach English.

Her name is Caroline. She's a little too pale for me. It's not that I don't fancy white girls, but she has the kind of skin which simply cannot tan. More matte than gloss. Her eyes make up for this though. The colour of shallow Maldivian sea.

She's wearing jeggings. JoJo catches me looking at her arse when she gets up to shake a new arrival's hand. He gives me the thumbs-up and then whispers to others, no doubt, that I am an arse-staring horndog bugger.

The intimate little dinner JoJo has arranged for me ends up with forty-six people. We are moved to a table outside, next to the fishpond. I can't say I would have invited all the people he has if I had been involved in the planning, but I guess the small talk does keep me busy enough to only text Aiya fourteen times to check on Kiki. When I ask him if she's breathing he doesn't reply, which makes me call him.

'Thought you were joking, *machang*,' he says.

I end up alone with Caroline after we share a bowl of red curry king prawns. We sit on the rocks by the pond, feeding fish about the size of Kiki's legs. We watch, through the trees, people younger than us swaying to music by the pool.

Caroline's two years out of uni, but more mature than I am. We talk about our favourite books; she reads three books a week. I impress her by saying that I read at least one a day, but I don't tell her the names of them, like *Who's in the Loo?*, *Hairy McClairy from Donaldson's Dairy* and *Dealing with Cancer* (which I dip into every night).

'You live alone?' I ask.

'Well yeah,' she says, 'but my landlady lives below and she's just got a puppy that sleeps in my room.'

'Oh, how sweet. What kind?'

'Cocker spaniel. Black.'

'My favourite,' I say.

'Yes, something to cuddle and kiss at night.'

At this point I could tell her about Kiki but I don't.

Gish, the fifty-year-old owner of Silk nightclub, joins us and starts talking about the TV series Caroline should watch.

'What's the first one I should get?' Caroline asks him.

Silent for a moment, Gish looks sideways as if to smell his own fart. '*Lie to Me*,' he says.

'You don't look a day over twenty,' she says.

It takes me a second to register the humour here, only because I don't know her well enough to ascertain whether she's a bland, straightforward, say-as-you-see-it kind of girl, or just a joker. Gish laughs, but moves to a different table without another word.

To make amends, we suggest to everyone that we go to Silk and while the others are whacking champagne inside, Caroline and I sit by the pool below, looking over a cricket pitch, sharing a bottle of white wine and a packet of Dunhill Lights.

The more I drink, the less plain she looks. I attribute her lack of stand-out features to an economy with make-up, and I like that. She doesn't wear lipstick or nail polish. Sometimes Menaka wore so much make-up she looked like a pantomime hooker.

Maybe in her plainness, Caroline is less up her own arse than Menaka is.

But I don't have the urge to hold the back of her head and pull her lips to mine; no urge to stick my tongue down her throat.

I hold Caroline's hand and that's all I try. It may look like I'm playing hard to get here, but unless you're Menaka, I am.

I'd love to be able to kiss Caroline just to say that I have. Just to convince myself that there is life after Menaka. But I'm not sure if there is.

Robin and his bird find us by the pool and they give me one smile between the two of them. The smile says, look we're here for you, but you're barking up the wrong tree with this chick.

Maybe their collective smile is right. I hug Robin and say into his ear, 'Get her home safely, please.'

I kiss Caroline on the cheeks. 'I'll text you.'

I drag my feet down the stairs, and it's just one of those things that happen next. One of those things you fear happening, especially in a small, incestuous place like Colombo. Menaka enters the nightclub complex, skidding around in some absurdly high heels, while Gayan holds her up by the arse.

It's too much. I run straight past them, not fast enough to escape their giggles.

In the tuk tuk on the way home, I text Caroline. 'Sorry I had to leave. I have a three-year-old daughter at home. Single father and all that. It was wonderful to meet you. Hope we can meet again and maybe you can invite me around to see your pussy.'

Her reply. 'For sure, but I hope you mean puppy'

Aiya is on the sofa, hugging a pillow and snoring, and Uncle Thilak is sprawled across the cut cement floor, his sarong bunched up around his waist, displaying something that looks like a barbecued one-legged octopus.

I pull his sarong down to cover his dignity, then check if he's breathing.

Aiya arches back like a cobra, the hair by his ears spread against the fan's breeze.

'What happened?' I ask, pointing at Uncle Thilak.

Jumping to his feet, Aiya says, 'Shit, he insisted on waiting up for you.'

I'm not really in a position to tell a son how to look after his father, but this is irresponsible of him.

'What's the time?' Aiya asks.

'Three-thirty.'

'We were drinking till about three-fifteen. Old bugger can still pack them in.'

'Should we call the doctor?' I ask. 'In case he had a fall.'

'He'd kill us if we did.'

'Let's get him to bed. Physio at nine.'

Aiya grabs Uncle Thilak by the wrists and I wrap my hands around his ankles. Literally, wrap. My fingers overlap my thumb.

Talk about deadweight. For a man that looks like he has zero fat and zero muscle on him, Uncle Thilak proves difficult to shift. Halfway up the stairs, I have to insist that we put him down and then Aiya asks if we can swap positions so that he doesn't have to walk backwards up the last few steps.

'Do you think we can drag him?' I ask. Half-joking, but also hopeful.

Aiya looks like he wants to agree but can't.

I take in three deep breaths. 'Ready.'

'One, two, three and step,' I say, again and again, till we get him on the landing upstairs, at which point Aiya and I collapse on our backs.

Uncle Thilak is up on his feet before I can open my eyes again. 'Thanks for that,' he says behind his crooked smile. 'Couldn't be bothered walking up the stairs myself.'

twenty

I cannot imagine how cancer must affect someone. How the disease must feel. But if I had to go on what Uncle Thilak is showing, it doesn't look all that bad.

His philosophy is not to change anything. He smokes, he drinks and he likes to think he plays golf, but the reality is that he goes to the golf club to smoke and drink. He takes a lot of pills and has a full-time nurse to follow him around, but she ends up doing more for Kiki than for him. In return, when he goes out with driver Ranjith, he buys his nurse chocolates and things for her children.

Maybe cancer makes you nicer. Or maybe it's the realisation that soon you will be just a memory.

He takes pills for the pain and to help him sleep, which he swallows with his favourite Scotch. His favourite Scotch? The cheapest one. He's too secure about himself now to worry about what others think.

In the morning, he looks much worse than at any other time. His eyes are bloodshot and the bags under them are packed, overweight and marked fragile. He is a little short with his compassion and words before eight in the morning, even with Kiki, which means that I have to make sure I am extra nice to both of them at those times.

If you didn't know better, you would simply think he wakes up with a hangover and nothing else. As bad as hangovers are, you can survive them, and even though I know he has less than six months left on the lifespan the doctors said he was restricted to, I really don't expect him to die. Ever.

The thing is, Aiya says that Uncle Thilak didn't mention death at all the first time he got cancer, but this time he is planning for it.

For instance, he insists that I go back to work. He has funded Kiki and me pretty much since she was born almost four years ago.

'The well will soon dry up, *suddha*,' he says. 'You white folk have lived off our jewels for a long time. No more. Make enough to educate Kiki. Send her to university. Do you have that pride, *suddha*?'

I do have some pride and I'm aware of the need to pay for Kiki. Of course I am, but the reason I have not given it as much thought as I should have is because I assumed Uncle Thilak would leave money for Kiki in his will. Being short of money has never crossed my mind.

'The house is worth a fair amount,' he says, 'but it's in Menaka's name. The second she needs it, you'll be turfed out.'

'Can I not contest it?'

'Well, quite frankly, you wouldn't want to. There's a one hundred per cent tax on foreigners owning land.'

I start thinking, my finger to my chin.

'You're wondering why she hasn't turfed you out already? Well because she'd have to look after Kiki then. And me.'

'No,' I say, 'actually I was wondering about how we could keep this house if it was in Kiki's name, since she is also Sri Lankan.'

*

So it's back to work for me, and thank God Jimmy Walsh rated my teaching ability and thank God he impregnated both the Economics teachers. I have been employed to cover their maternity leave and am allowed to come and go as and when I have classes. Except for Thursdays, when I teach till 3.20, and Uncle Thilak comes with the driver to drop and pick up Kiki from the school's nursery section.

As a father, of course I am concerned about how Kiki will grow up. I don't want to spoil her and make her demanding. I don't want her to think she can always get her way.

Uncle Thilak has no such issues.

So Thursday is Kiki's day to be spoilt silly and she loves it.

Normally, Uncle Thilak takes her to Water's Edge to walk around and see the rabbits and the deer. Then he buys her cakes and salty caramel ice cream at the Good Market afterwards. Then they go shopping, and she always has an expensive toy and a new hat to show off to me.

Today, when I come home, Kiki is pouring sugar into the garden for some reason.

'Baby,' I say, 'you mustn't waste food. Imagine all the starving children in Africa.'

'Well, they're not going to come to our place for sugar, are they?'

The sort of smart arse thing Uncle Thilak would say.

I distract her by picking up our four tortoises from out of a bush and placing them in the middle of the lawn. As always, she pats their shells and then lines them up as if for a race.

'Where'd you go today?' I ask.

One tortoise sets off early so she picks him up and puts him back at the starting line. 'Seeya took me to see orphans.'

I have to take in a very deep breath and keep it in there, squeezing the tension out of my muscles. 'An orphanage?'

'Yes, Daddy, it was loads of fun.'

'You played with them?'

She nodded.

'You touched them?'

'Hugged them, Daddy. Hugged them.'

Ugh. I go out of my way to make sure she's lice-free. I keep her from touching her friends even, so she doesn't get their germs, and now in the space of a few hours her head has probably become a lice festival and she may contract warts and some virus.

'Where is he?' I ask her. 'Where's Seeya?'

'Putting a nap.'

She is speaking like him too. 'How many did you hug?'

'All, Daddy. Seeya said those buggers have no one to love. No mummy or daddy.'

She said buggers? I grab her and put her on my lap, searching her hair for lice. 'Did you eat anything there?'

'No, Daddy. Seeya took me to KFC before.' Kiki turns around on my lap and hugs me. Probably giving me lice, but a hug is rare from a girl who does not like showing affection, so I accept it.

'Seeya told me how lucky I am to have a daddy.'

That old bugger. Because of him I almost cry, but I fight it. No way can I succumb.

'He told me never to forget how lucky I am.'

'Me too,' I say.

'Daddy, can we go to Odel? I want to buy some toys for those buggers –'

'Baba, that's a bad word.'

'Odel?' she asks.

'No, the other word.' I don't know how to explain which one without saying it. 'Never mind. Yes, we can go to Odel.'

'Good, because those buggers don't have anyone to buy them toys. I have you and Seeya.'

I pull her head into my chest and stroke her hair. 'Yes, you do.'

After Kiki is asleep, I want to say something nice to Uncle Thilak.

We're on the veranda drinking our arrack. I'm on the hammock, the glass resting on my tummy as I rock from side to side. He's on his planter's chair, his legs extended in front of him.

We watch a monkey leap from one tree and catch a palm leaf of another, and outside the gate we hear street dogs screech in pain as they fight over territory.

I want to tell Uncle Thilak how moved I am about what he said to Kiki and the lesson he taught her. But we just don't have that kind of relationship, so instead I say, 'Please, could you not teach my daughter to say bugger all the time?'

'Why, you bugger?' he says. 'It may be a bad word in *suddha* land, but your daughter is a Sri Lankan.' He puffs out his chest as he says this. 'And she should be proud of it. Here bugger just means chap.'

I hold my hand over my mouth and bow my head. 'Thank you for what you told her.'

'What's that, *suddha*?' he asks. 'My hearing is not what it once was.'

'Never mind,' I say. 'I just, you know, I'm just grateful that you stepped up to the plate when Menaka left.'

'Don't go crying on me, little girl,' he says. 'You couldn't have done it without me. Blah blah blah. Yes I know. You drove my daughter out of my life, you white prick, but at least you gave me Kiki.'

twenty-one

I want to crash my car into the stupid tuk tuks driving on the wrong side of the road. They weave in and out of traffic as if they are motorcycles, turning without looking into their mirrors, using their pathetic little horns to be aggressive.

It's not just them. Jimmy Walsh called me about the reports I sent out; for Pradeep in the Lower Sixth, I meant to say, 'All the other students are very fond of him.' Instead, I wrote, 'All the other students are very fond of me.' Jimmy saw the funny side of it and said it was right up there with P.D.L.D.R Silva's cricket report for Jeevan: 'Enthusiasm excellent. Talent zero.'

Funny, maybe, but I don't like being caught out for mistakes.

Add to this the fact that Caroline, my best female friend, which I think I can now safely call her since we spend all our breaks together, is rumoured to have a boyfriend. Since she is no longer available, this makes her much more attractive than I had previously thought.

I have Robin on speakerphone and he fills me in on the latest news in Colombo nightlife. He tells me that Caroline has been seen with Sujeewa Manawaduge, the left-arm fast bowler just picked for Sri Lanka. It hurts me more than it should. I tell Robin I'm cool. Good the girl has a man, you know, that kind of thing. He says he was surprised to see them together because it's so obvious that she's in love with me.

'Rubbish, mate,' I say. 'She's just lonely.'

'Mate, she watches cricket with you. She hates cricket.'

I didn't realise anyone hated cricket, so if that's the only evidence he has, I don't buy it.

I drive through our gates almost hitting Kiki, who is pushing Uncle Thilak in his wheelchair down the cobblestone path.

I want to yell, but instead I put off the engine and listen.

Kiki's heavy steps, fast, almost too fast, suggest that she is losing control.

'Darling, slow down a bit please,' Uncle Thilak says.

'No Seeya, that lizard will eat you.'

In the middle of the lawn, a two-foot-long monitor lizard appears to be more interested in sunbathing than consuming a bony old man.

'Darling, don't forget the well at the end of the garden,' Uncle Thilak says. 'Don't push me in there. Maybe enough now, baba.'

'The lizard wants to eat you, Seeya.'

'Kiki, Bo Bo,' I say.

She turns her head, letting go of the wheelchair as she falls to the grass. The wheelchair is on a very slight slope but I manage to catch up with it, shifting it to the side to stop it from rolling further, then run back to Kiki who is up on her feet, dusting off her knees. She adopts her karate pose and stares down the lizard.

'Save Seeya, Daddy.' A vein bulges on her neck. 'I'll watch the lizard. You save Seeya.'

'Darling, the lizard's not paying us any attention.'

Without taking her eyes off the lizard, she points to the right. 'Go, go, go.'

I do as I'm told and get Seeya onto the elevated veranda and then come back for Kiki. I try to lift her onto my shoulders, but she pushes my hands away.

'That's okay,' she says. 'The lizard only wants Seeya.'

After Kiki is asleep, Uncle Thilak explains himself. Kiki asked him why he can no longer walk, and rather than admit that he can, but that the cancer has made him very weak, he told her that a massive lizard bit his ankles.

This could be him losing his mind, but to be honest, it's the kind of thing he would have said at the best of times.

The lizard may not be eating away at him as we speak, but the cancer is.

I knew this, not when he started using a wheelchair, but when he stopped smoking.

I'm sitting next to an ashtray now. There is a lit cigarette in it, and a glass of cold beer by its side, both for Uncle Thilak. But he doesn't touch either.

After his last operation a week ago, everything hurts his mouth, even the effervescent vitamin C tablets I try to give him after reading a book that suggested excessive doses could cure cancer. At times like these, you believe anything.

Uncle Thilak thinks I am trying to keep him alive so that the money keeps flowing, but I don't care. Maybe there is some truth in that, but there's also so much more.

It's not worth imagining how sad Kiki will be when Uncle Thilak leaves us.

It may or may not be a good thing that I am inebriated at the staff dinner. I have to seize the moment, and I know this is the only time I can be sure to be with Caroline when her boyfriend isn't there.

I just straight up come out with it and ask her about him. She tells me they're taking things slowly; maybe they are boyfriend and girlfriend, maybe they aren't. But he's really good to her. She shows me his photograph and reminds me that the first time she ever saw him was while watching cricket with me. I'm a fan and an advocate of him playing regularly for Sri Lanka. The picture represents him well. His face is dark in places, darker in others and his nose spans across his cheeks.

'I could park my car in his nostrils,' I say.

Bit of a conversation killer.

I'm in a taxi, dropping Caroline home. I turn to her. It's a struggle, but I manage to speak clearly enough through my slurring.

Remembering Menaka's lines, I ask, 'Do you like Prince?'

'The singer?'

'The singer, yes.'

'A little.'

'How do you like "If I was your Girlfriend"?'

Shit, I just realised it doesn't work this way around.

'The song?'

I nod.

'Yeah, it's all right.'

'Yes, it is.' I hold her hand. 'I'm happy for you, but I'm jealous.'

I can feel her hand tightening around mine.

'Why?' She's smiling. A good sign.

'I didn't realise how much I fancied you.' I want to lift up her skirt and stroke her white legs. I hope I didn't say that aloud.

'Don't be silly,' she says. 'You're just winding me up.'

I hold the back of her neck and she doesn't stop me. I kiss her cheek and her ear, and stop. 'Sorry,' I say.

'I fancied the pants off you, Eddie.' She touches my thigh. 'But you knew that, obviously, and did nothing about it so I gave up on you.'

'But I didn't know. Until now,' I say.

She leans across and kisses me on the cheek and then on my lips. We slide down the backseat.

✶

I wake up as the sun rises outside my bedroom. My bamboo blinds are up, allowing a monkey to stare at me.

The girl on my mind?

It's Caroline. Oh boy, it's Caroline, not Menaka, and I wonder if she can get out to my house today to go further than a snog.

It's not as if we don't know each other. No need to play games.

I text: 'That was amazing. I'm so glad we talked and did that. Now you know how much I fancy you.'

She replies: 'I have to admit I loved that, but it was a mistake. I'm sorry. I'm not the kind of person to cheat on my boyfriend. Can we pretend that never happened?'

My teeth have been ripped out. My testicles slammed into a drawer. My nose and mouth taped shut. That's how I feel.

'Dada, I'm awake,' Kiki says into the baby monitor.

twenty-two

I play along. Let's be friends, I tell Caroline. Let's forget what happened. Go back to how we were.

She calls me her best friend, still, which I like; it means I'm a better friend than her boyfriend.

When school opens again, I spend as much time with her as he does. So she says. He trains long hours. Gets home late. Tours the island, other countries. Lives with his parents so Caroline can't stay the night.

I'm at school more than I used to be. Uncle Thilak is happy to have one extra day a week to spoil Kiki. He takes her out on Wednesdays, driven by Ranjith. Sometimes Aiya goes with them; at least two nurses, at all times. Uncle Thilak is now being fed pureed food through a tube, so he needs constant care. His speech is very unclear to anyone but me, so sometimes I'm called to translate what he says to the maid.

At school I help Caroline with her reports, carry her books to her car, touch her arm, her leg. I think I'm finally over Menaka.

I know the school staff mocks me. They know I'm after her. They know she's not available. Or maybe they mock her. For two-timing. Maybe they mock Sujeewa Manawaduge, the international superstar, whose white bird likes white bits.

If I can't win Caroline over, maybe Kiki can. I pick her up from nursery and bring her to the senior section of the school. She asks Caroline if she would like to come to our house.

Caroline says yes straightaway. Maybe I should have asked earlier. She's lonely, I think. Her boyfriend (I hate saying that) is playing in Bangladesh for two weeks.

While Kiki has her afternoon nap, I share a bottle of white with Caroline on our yoga deck – unused for yoga since Menaka left. Used twice before she left.

'Kiki makes me want to rush home,' I say.

'She's so gorgeous.'

'You know, cricketers are famous for cheating on tour. Some of them, I'm not naming names, never had female attention before and now that they do, they can't turn it down.'

Caroline laughs. 'Are you suggesting Sujeewa is doing that?'

'I didn't say that.'

'Nice try, mate,' she says.

'I guess I just move on to plan B,' I say.

She leans forward in her chair. 'Am I still plan A?'

'Today, yes, tomorrow, who knows?'

'You have someone else in mind?' she asks.

Like a child, I draw an imaginary zip across my lips. Caroline downs her wine and reaches for the cigarette packet Uncle Thilak left here last night.

'You don't smoke,' I say.

Her coughing, after the first drag, confirms this.

'Sujeewa wanted me from the moment he met me. Not just when he thought I was unattainable.'

'I didn't want to mess with our friendship.'

She shakes her head and grins. 'I know we'd be a better match. But...'

I massage her thigh over her jeans. 'But?'

'You deserve someone else. I can't make you wait for me because that day may never come.'

I down my drink and open another bottle of wine.

We sit in silence until Kiki comes out. Our new black cocker spaniel's on the loose, but Kiki has her collar and lead in her hands.

Caroline goes out to my daughter and squats next to her, smiling. I can't hear what she's saying.

I lean forward and hold my face in my hands. Close my eyes. Think about texting Menaka. Think about texting the hot girl from my neighbouring boarding school. My first love.

Kiki is screaming. I look up.

She has the dog's collar around Caroline's wrist. They are jogging beside each other, as if Kiki is taking Caroline for a run.

They delight in this.

Caroline sits on the lawn. Shakes hands. Rolls over. Kiki is bouncing up and down.

This is the moment, I think; I have found Kiki's new mother. That sounds psychotic, I know. But especially with Uncle Thilak on the way out, Kiki needs another caregiver.

So do I.

Caroline sneaks off to the end of the veranda to make a phone call. She tries to cover her mouth with her hand, but I can see that she's having a heated discussion with someone. She puts the phone in her pocket.

'Problem?' I ask

'Not really. Sujeewa's angry that I didn't answer his calls before, but he does that to me all the time.'

'You ignored his call?'

'Kiki insisted,' Caroline says. 'And she doesn't strike me as the kind of gal you can say no to.'

'Then I hope she asked you to stay for dinner.'

'And a bath. But I don't think I can share a bath with both of you like she wanted.'

'Her bath?'

'And story time. She wants me to read to her because she says she's having trouble understanding her Seeya these days.'

'You're okay with that?'

'Yes, and if you're okay with it, she wants me to read to her in the tree house.'

I smile myself into, what I assume to be, a very goofy look. This is a fantasy come true for me. Can it happen? Will Kiki and I have someone to share our life with? Someone who will put Kiki to bed sometimes, who will read to her, bathe her. Love her. I'm getting ahead of myself.

The plan for Caroline's next visit is to order the most kickass Thai meal known to civilised man. When you need to know what to order and where from in Colombo, you call Kenneth McAlpine, which is what I do. The food arrives just after Caroline does, but I can't get her to the dinner table because she's too busy painting with Kiki. So I just lean back on the veranda, light a mosquito coil and watch them. To my left, Uncle Thilak rolls himself back and forth in his wheelchair. His face is scrunched up, looking angry, looking disturbed that his time with Kiki has been taken away. He moves his wheelchair nearer to the veranda stairs. Teasing them almost. I know what he's doing. He's trying to get attention. Trying to get one of us to run up to him and say be careful.

But, as if he is a child, I think it's best to ignore him.

He nudges closer, the front of his wheels protruding over the drop of the first terracotta-tiled step.

'Uncle,' I say. 'We spent enough time at hospital today without having to think about a repeat visit, don't you think?'

His little wrists flick the chair back a bit. But then forward again.

'Uncle,' I say. Shout, really. Kiki and Caroline look up at me and then I see their hands to their faces and I can't hear anything.

Caroline runs to the veranda; Uncle Thilak is sprawled on the lawn, his wheelchair collapsed beside him.

Then the sounds: Kiki crying. Caroline calling my name. Nothing from Uncle Thilak.

I run down the stairs, dropping to my knees besides him.

'Seeya, Seeya,' Kiki says.

I see the blood gushing out of his head.

'Please take her upstairs,' I say. 'Can you manage that?'

'Of course.' Caroline scoops Kiki up in her arms.

'Is Seeya okay?' Kiki asks, but she doesn't try to fight her way out of Caroline's grip.

I strip off my T-shirt and press it against Uncle Thilak's head to try to stop the bleeding, and then I feel his hand on mine.

'Why the hell didn't you stop me, *suddha*?' he asks.

'You're okay?'

With my help, he turns onto his back and looks up at me. I wipe blood off his forehead before it drips into his eyes.

'Of course I'm not okay, you jackass. You let me fall down eight steps.'

'You need stitches,' I say.

'You need a heart,' he says.

I lean back so I can shout up to Kiki's room. 'Everything okay up there?'

Caroline comes to the balcony.

'What is this?' Uncle Thilak asks. 'Some tropical Romeo and Juliet bullshit?'

I lift a palm towards his face to get him to be quiet.

'Don't you bloody raise your hand to me,' he says.

So I try to talk over him: 'I have to take him for some stitches. Can you manage her for an hour?'

'Of course,' she says.

'Can't thank you enough.'

'Oh, get a room,' Uncle Thilak says.

Uncle Thilak needs three stitches, which he accepts with the proviso that the doctor makes him look like Amitabh Bachchan by the end of it.

The doctor fails to deliver and Uncle Thilak pretends to be upset.

By the time we get back, there is a taxi waiting in my driveway; Caroline is sitting on the veranda, the baby monitor in her hand. Uncle Thilak has passed out in the car so I leave him there for a moment, with the door open.

'She's asleep?' I ask.

She nods, standing as she does so.

'How'd you do that so easily?' I thought I was the only person (well, and Uncle Thilak) who could do that.

'Pretty simple.' Caroline smiles. 'I have to go, I'm afraid.'

'But did you eat?'

'Maybe you can save me some.' She closes her eyes and shakes her head. 'Sujeewa's been calling and he's pretty irate I'm not at home.'

'He's on tour, isn't he?'

She nods. 'Yes, but rather than lying to him about where I am, I just have to get back to my landline. We're fighting all the time these days.'

That's bad news for her, maybe, but good for me.

After Caroline leaves, I get Uncle Thilak into bed and call JoJo and Kenny over to whack the Thai food, but we end up getting 'cockered' and forget to eat.

The third time she comes, Caroline gives me some wonderful news.

Under the light of the full moon, she's on the hammock tied between two of our palm trees and I am lying under it.

I feel one of her tears drop on my face.

'We've broken up,' she says. 'At least, we're on a break. I said I needed space to see where we were going.'

'You and me?' I ask.

'No, me and him,' she says. 'Me and him. I'm confused. I think I probably need to be alone for now.'

Is she breaking up with me? How can she, if we're not in a relationship? This is the first time I have been dumped by someone else's girlfriend.

'Can I stay here tonight?' she asks. 'But just as friends?'

'For sure,' I say. 'For sure.'

'I think I need a hug.' She smiles at me. 'But nothing else, right?'

Uncle Thilak insists on joining us for a drink. His desperation is such that he is willing to endure the pain in his mouth since I plain refused to pour whisky down the tube in his chest.

'So tell me, miss, what brings you to Sri Lanka?' he asks.

'The experience of working in another country.'

'You like it here?'

'Absolutely love it,' she says.

'Your tippex skin can cope with the sun?'

Caroline looks at me, her eyebrows raised. 'Um, yes, fine.'

'Do you drive here, lady?' Uncle Thilak asks.

'No, not yet, because I don't have a car but Eddie said he'd teach me.'

'Not a bloody hope. You won't be able to drive on our roads. You're too frail.'

Caroline looks at me. 'Is he always this charming?'

'Just for special guests,' I say, 'and by special I mean white.'

༄

Uncle Thilak nods off in his planter's chair in his sarong, his legs extended wide enough for me to have to make Caroline move so she doesn't see something she'd wish she hadn't.

I take her upstairs, show her to our open rain shower, give her one of my T-shirts. By the time I get back downstairs, Uncle Thilak is burping himself awake, so I put his arm over my shoulder and walk him up to his room. He wants to check on Kiki on the way, kissing her on the cheek, almost falling on top of her, before backing away and closing the door behind himself.

'One whisky for the road,' he says.

'There is no road,' I say. 'Your room's right here.'

'One for the room then. Or would you like me to bug you all night?'

On a normal day I would have said no, but I am desperate to get to Caroline before she falls asleep.

'Straight whisky?' I ask.

'No, *suddha*,' he says. 'I'd like a homosexual one please.'

I give him a glass full of whisky and go back to my room where I crack open another bottle of red to share with Caroline.

My mind strays a little and I wonder if she will accept a bit of fondling into the hugging package, but I endeavour to behave myself.

Easier said than done when she slips off the bathrobe to get into bed with me and she wears only an old T-shirt.

I behave myself. I know I shouldn't take advantage of her now that she has drunk so much. But I want to. Goddammit, I want to, but I must think long term. Respect.

I roll away from her and face the wall. But I feel her body press against my back. Her tongue in my ear. Down my neck. Her hands are under my T-shirt. On my chest. I turn to her. There is enough light from the full moon outside for me to see the outline of her face. A brown Caroline. We move our heads together. My hand strays to her legs. Up them, exploring, seeing how far I will be allowed to go, and she moans.

Bang. Caroline bolts upright. Bang bang bang. Thuds so loud they wake Kiki, who starts calling out for me through the baby monitor in her room.

I jump out of bed and scurry to the door, unlocking it.

I lift my hands to my face in defence when I see Uncle Thilak, standing at the door, no wheelchair, his eyes as if they've been soaked in chlorine. Like Jack Nicholson from the *Shining*.

'Tell that white tart to get out of my house,' he says.

I can't speak. I try to hold my hand to his mouth, but he sways away, probably more by drunken accident than design. 'Tell that bitch to get out of my daughter's room.'

'Uncle, shut up,' I say. 'Shut up.'

'It's okay,' Caroline says. 'I better go.'

'She's screwing Sujeewa Manawaduge behind your back.'

'That's her boyfriend.'

Caroline pulls up her jeans and gathers the rest of her clothes, as she approaches the door. 'I'll give you back your T-shirt at school,' she says. 'Excuse me.'

She is almost past Uncle Thilak when he grabs at her arm.

'Get off me, you creep,' she says.

'You bloody white slut coming to our country and thinking you can steal other women's men.'

'Get off me.' She wrestles her arm free and marches towards the stairs.

'You're just after our money. Like a cheap hooker.'

Caroline turns on her heel and charges back at Uncle Thilak, a hand raised to slap him. He tries to get out of the way, but stumbles over his weak and drunken legs. His head crashes against the door handle.

Collapsing onto the ground, blood pours out of his head like oil from a ruptured pipeline. I drop to my knees but Caroline is there first. Her blouse to his head. Trying to stop the blood.

'Uncle,' I say. Ten times or more. No response.

Kiki comes into the corridor and Caroline holds a hand up. 'Stop, Kiki, darling. I'll come to your room and sleep there. Daddy has to take Uncle Thilak to the doctor.'

Caroline's thumb and little finger go to her ear. I nod and mouth, yes, I'll call.

I don't want to wake up Ranjith or the nurses. There's no way of knowing what abuse Uncle Thilak will hurl at them and he wouldn't want to be seen like this. I carry him to the car, cradled in my arms like a newborn baby. He doesn't weigh a great deal more than Kiki now.

I wrap his head in a tea towel, and roll brown tape around it. The bleeding worries me.

I can get to Hemas Hospital in about four minutes at this time of night, so there's no point being too fancy. I call our neighbour who works as an accountant at the hospital and ask her if she can ring in and tell them to be ready for me. I beep the horn as I get through the hospital's gate and when I screech my car to a stop outside emergency, there are two nurses and a wheelchair waiting for Uncle Thilak.

They tell me to park. They'll stitch him up.

I haven't seen two nurses run so fast since Uncle Thilak made his nurses race for a bet.

I throw my keys to a security guard and promise him I'll come back to park my car as soon as I can, but I know I can't leave Uncle Thilak, even though I just want to give him an almighty slap for the way he was behaving.

His head rolls around as they lift him onto a table. One nurse strokes his hand, smiles at him, and says, 'Aney sweet fellow.'

She obviously can't understand what he is saying. Only I can. Fortunately.

'Tell this *junglee* not to touch my hand,' he says. 'And you can bugger off. Bloody traitor. Bringing a hooker to your wife's bed. Bitch tried to kill me. I'll have that whore deported.'

I smile. That's all I can do. I want to leave him there. Let him die if that's what's going to happen. They inject him with something I assume to be pain relief, but I don't really care what it is. He drifts off to sleep as they stitch the cut on his head.

I go park my car and call Caroline to tell her that the nurses have said he must stay overnight for observation. She offers to watch over Kiki, which I am grateful for, but I suggest that once Uncle Thilak is checked into a room I will come home. By the time I get back inside, Uncle Thilak is awake, although his eyes are like marbles rolling around a bowl. I am asked to swipe my credit card at the cashier for check-in, so I wheel the old bastard with me. He looks so gentle. So harmless.

He is inches behind me when I lean over the cashier's counter.

Once I have paid, I turn to get him, but he is not there. I gather my receipt and sprint around the corner to see the little old man pumping his arms, like oil drills, his wheelchair moving at quite a lick.

He's trying to get out the main exit. This is like Kiki attempting to get into a room she knows she's not allowed to enter without me.

A nurse runs out and stops him.

I fear for what he will say to her.

Sprinting at full pelt, I skid past him, across the last bit of polished floor. I turn, dreading the worst. But he has his hands up, palms together in prayer. Begging the nurse to let him go home but he can't speak. So he points. Like Kiki used to do to tell us which toy she wanted.

He's pointing to the car. To the road, and in the vague direction of my house.

When he sees me, he smiles as if nothing has happened, and I am pretty sure in his mind nothing has. 'Kiki,' he says. 'Kiki, Kiki, Kiki.'

※

Uncle Thilak sleeps well, and when he wakes, he points to the window. 'Who's with Kiki?'

I'm reluctant to tell him the woman who he thinks is a whore is with his darling granddaughter. 'She's okay.'

'That blonde girl is with her?'

I nod, my gaze darting away from him.

'That's good,' he says. 'She seems to love Kiki.'

Who *is* this man?

I assume he has no recollection of anything that happened, but on the way home he asks me to stop the car outside a shop that sells antique furniture. In the window are two dolls of an old man and an old woman, both white, rocking on miniature chairs.

The shop owner responds to Uncle Thilak waving him over. He comes to our car and tells us the dolls are over seventy years old, made for an English tea-planter and his wife. Collector's items. Very expensive.

Uncle Thilak wants them, but he has no wallet on him so I have to pay out of funds saved for Kiki.

⌇

Caroline is on the veranda having a tea party with Kiki. 'Look, it's Seeya,' she says. Her smile is as genuine as one could expect in the circumstances.

I leave Uncle Thilak in the back of the car while I run to lift up Kiki. She wraps her arms around me, her fingers tapping my back as if playing the piano.

'Daddy, Daddy, Caroline and I had a midnight feast.' She looks over my shoulder, pushes out of my arms and runs to the car. 'Seeya, Seeya, Seeya.' She slams her palms against the car door, and when I open it for her, she climbs onto Uncle Thilak's lap and kisses him on the head, very close to his bandaged wound. 'I love you, Seeya.'

Caroline moves in to kiss me on the cheeks but I back away.

'I haven't washed for ages.' I reach out for her hand. 'But if you don't mind –'

'Let's wait till you shower.' She turns away from me. 'How is the old bastard?'

'Caroline,' Uncle Thilak says. 'Caroline.' He curls his fingers to call her over.

I am pretty sure if not for Kiki, Caroline would have served him with a few choice swear words; instead, she ambles towards him. But she isn't near enough to satisfy the old man and he grabs her hand and tries to drag her in closer. He says something in her ear. When Caroline backs away, she has the box of dolls and rocking chairs Uncle Thilak bought.

I help Uncle Thilak into his wheelchair and his nurse pushes him up the ramp to his room to bathe him. Kiki follows them.

'What did he say?' I ask.

'He gave me this,' she says. 'Says it's you and me growing old together.'

twenty-three

Caroline is still on a break from Sujeewa. I believe her, mainly because I've checked on her, watched her Facebook page, her Twitter account. I know where she is most of the time.

But still. Can't she just give up on that punk and let him focus on his cricket and nostril hair grooming?

As it stands, we are still just friends. I wonder if that would have been any different if Uncle Thilak hadn't attacked her that night. You would have to think that served as a bit of a turn-off. I considered seeing if we could find a nursing home for him, but whatever said and done, whatever he does, he is still Kiki's grandfather and she loves him.

Caroline's getting a little more used to Uncle Thilak. She accepts him. Laughs off his abuse when it comes, because she knows he's heavily on drugs to mask his pain.

Yesterday he claimed he saw her dressed as a Klansman.

She thinks he's hallucinating, which is possible, sure, but I think he's being mischievous. At least now that he can't drink he is no longer an angry amazing racist.

Today, when she comes into his room to say hello, he looks confused. He stares at her; watches her move around the room. When she tries to hold his wrist he lets her, but after a while he pulls it away, looks at it, explores it. Like Kiki did with her hand, when she first discovered she could move it herself.

He looks at me. He always knows me, but he doesn't smile.

I think he may have about five crooked smiles left in him each day, and four of those are reserved for Kiki and one for Daisy, the cocker spaniel. Poor Daisy fights to get out of his hugs whenever she can, and often I have to roll him off her to make sure that she hasn't suffocated.

🌿

Menaka is here on one of her fleeting visits. I moan to Caroline that she shows interest in her father only to ensure her inheritance, but I know it's more than that. Somewhere in that machine is a heart and I think she loves Uncle Thilak.

Caroline points out that any changes made to his will now could be contested anyway as he's not in sound mind.

Gayan is still on the scene, but doesn't come with Menaka to our house, which is good. I feel his influence. Much as Uncle Thilak and Aiya had warned me. There's just something too guarded about Menaka.

That is, until I get a text from her after she has left the house, asking me if I will have a drink with her tonight at the Colombo Swimming Club.

I think about asking Caroline if she minds, but why should I? She's made no commitment to me, and for all I know she's meeting Sujeewa tonight anyway. Except I do know that she's not, because her Facebook page suggests she's having the girls over for dinner (which she told me herself too).

🌿

I am so nervous about meeting Menaka that I get to the Swimming Club early to have a few drinks with Jimmy and JoJo.

We amble down the stairs to the lawn where we sit with our backs to the colonial Storm Lodge. We're sheltered under a thatched roof, the sun setting over us towards the Indian Ocean.

Three Australian girls share our table, two of whom are long-limbed, flat-stomached and sharp-featured; the third isn't. I converse with the plump one, whose sunburnt skin peels off her bare shoulders like damp wallpaper.

Southern-bound trains stutter by between the club walls and the sea. The rusty mechanics of the engines drown out what we have to say, allowing us to concentrate on drinking and within minutes of arriving, I am on my third arrack.

The Australian girls wave at the passengers who hang out the train windows. Passengers who are poorer than us despite working much harder. By looking into the club, they're hoping to catch glimpses of another life; a life where women with red skin flaunt deep cleavage and the curves of chubby legs.

The arrack begins to kick in. It feels bloody good or a little sickening. I'm not sure.

The hired band howl out the words to 'Hotel California', backed by a pre-recorded beat on the electric organ.

I don't know how much I have drunk, but I should know better than to pull out the air guitar at what is, essentially, a family club. My dancing does its own job of creating future regret, but the girls I am with nod along, only the whites of their eyes showing, as if they have embraced a mystical local culture.

I con myself into believing I am high on something natural, allowing my head to rock in the breeze like the coconuts above me. I want to be lost in the moment, to be the white guy with the power of meditation, the guru of relaxation, the king of cool.

My arms hang limp by my sides, my legs float above the sand of the dance floor. I close my eyes and suck in the sticky sea air.

And in that moment, I am a child again. Hiding my anxieties, hiding the fear of what I think Menaka will say.

JoJo taps me on the shoulder and points up to the clubhouse. Out of the lights, the silhouette can only be Menaka's. The small waist, the muscular legs, the upturn of the chin.

We sit on wooden chairs, on a level above the pool bar from where Jimmy Walsh and JoJo wave to us.

I sip on an arrack and Diet Coke. Menaka has a pineapple juice. Measured as ever.

'You know the house is in my name, don't you?' she asks.

I nod. The bitch. I knew this was coming.

'Well, I haven't asked you to vacate it because I knew Thathi needed somewhere to stay.'

'You could have stayed with him if you cared.'

'Let's not be childish here,' she says. 'It's worth a lot of money and there's no reason why I should just give it away.'

'You'd turf your daughter out of the house she has grown up in?'

She swivels the straw around in her pineapple juice, takes a deep breath and closes her eyes. 'Well, that's just it. I am her mother and a girl needs her mother.'

I want to poke the bitch's eyes out. If she thinks for a fraction of a second that I will give up Kiki, she's a lunatic.

'What are you saying?' I ask, calling over a waiter and signalling for another drink.

'Sri Lankan law is on my side. I wouldn't have thought it's in your interest to contest this.'

'I ask again, what are you saying?'

'I think I'm ready to bring up Kiki.'

I straighten my legs out, knocking the table and our glasses over. Silence around the club. Everyone staring at me.

Waiters, swimmers, drinkers, passengers on a passing train.

'You try to take her from me and I will kill you. I swear on my life, I will kill you.'

Jimmy Walsh sprints up the steps and grabs my arms. JoJo, panting, follows him. They drag me through the clubhouse.

'What the hell's the matter with you?' Jimmy asks. 'You've lost the bloody plot.'

'She wants to take Kiki from me.'

Jimmy says, 'Well, you're not bloody helping yourself.'

I try to break out of their grip. I want one last rant at Menaka, but Jimmy, the piece of shit, knees me in the nuts.

I hunch to the floor. Squatting, my hands around my balls. He's my boss, I remember and this is excruciating pain.

'Sorry, Eddie,' he says. 'But you made me do that. Made me hurt you before you screwed everything up for yourself.'

'My driver's going to take you home, Eddie boy,' JoJo says.

I need to speak to someone who can talk Menaka out of this. She doesn't give a shit about Kiki. She's doing this for the wrong reasons.

I push Uncle Thilak across the dirt path between the paddy fields. His head is locked to one side, but occasionally he lifts a hand to point at a bird asking me what it is. Regardless of whether they are bright yellow, green or dull brown, I say they are the Ceylon Small Barbet as that is the only name I know.

He signals for me to stop pushing him.

'I warned you, *suddha*, but you never listen. White bastards like you patronise us browns without even knowing it. Can't credit us with thinking of something you didn't. I warned you. Told you to take action long ago. Now it's too late.'

'But you can speak to her, Uncle, please.'

'*Suddha*, I have a few months left. Last thing I want to do is fight with my daughter.'

'But this is for Kiki.' I swivel the wheelchair around and grab his arms, rattling his bones. 'Sorry, but I'm desperate.'

'Always have been,' he says. 'Now get your sweaty hands off me.'

'You know Kiki's better off with me.'

'I'm beginning to have my doubts. You're losing control.'

'Please,' I say.

Uncle Thilak pulls at my wrists so he can get onto his feet. 'I'm in too much pain, white boy. I'm in too much bloody pain.'

He insists on walking back to the house, but since he can barely move he gives up after twelve minutes. We are still on the dirt path, maybe fifteen feet from where he got out of his chair.

❧

Aiya agrees to meet me in a tavern off Galle Road. I get there before him, and assume that I am in the wrong place because this is a hang-out for trishaw drivers and off-duty beggars. When Aiya confirms I'm at the right place, I realise that this must have been his haunt at times when he had no money because he refused to dance to Uncle Thilak's tune.

It's dark and hard to see much further than the lit end of the cigarette in my mouth. The bar is circular and in the middle of the square room. Dotted around are cubicles that can fit six people each. I can't tell if the couches are dirty because there is no light, but they smell of damp socks. I don't see rats but I can hear them squeaking.

When Aiya comes through the door, he nudges me towards a table but I have to peel my flip flops from the floor which is sticky from spilt drinks.

A guy called Sunil serves Aiya an arrack and me a coffee that has the texture of dissolved mud.

'I could have told you this would happen,' he says. 'Gayan's the most dangerous kind of prick there is. A clever coward with no morals.'

'Is it the money they're after? I can just let them have the money if it's left to Kiki.'

'Offer that, if you're sure. But it can't be that simple. Thathi probably set up a trust so no one has access to the full amount. That's what Menaka must think. I don't know.'

'But Uncle Thilak will leave Menaka something, right?'

'The house you live in. That's what he told her. Anything in her name is hers to keep but she won't get anything else. The inheritance is, I think, to be split between me and Kiki.'

'Surely we can work something out. Of course I want Kiki to have what's hers but there's no way I'm giving her up. How can the legal system let her contest this when she has abandoned her?'

'Technically, you're still married?'

'Well, yes, but...'

'So say she starts divorce proceedings now, the issue of Kiki comes up for the first time.'

'Why now?' I ask. But I know the answer.

'Thathi never loses. If Thathi wanted you to keep Kiki, you would keep Kiki; Menaka challenging that would simply piss him off. This is all Gayan's doing, I tell you. Thathi's too weak now and Gayan knows it.'

I have to catch Gayan so I go to his gym. I follow an instructor up cracked steps. We enter a free-weights room. The atmosphere is raw and pumping; aggressive, yet friendly; rusty weights, yet order to everything. Wrinkled black and white posters on the wall of white men lifting more weights. The smell of sweat; the creaky fans that spit leaking water from broken pipes.

This all seems too try-hard, even by Gayan's standards. He could afford an air-conditioned Colombo 7 gym but he thinks he's hip. He's still a bar body: huge chest and arms, but feeble legs. Like toothpicks.

I have a speech planned, but when I see how smug he looks, my eyes well up. I get on my knees.

'I can't lose my baby,' I say. 'Please, please understand.'

He laughs. Taps his gym buddy on the back. 'You're bloody pathetic.'

'Please, I beg you, just think of what I'm going through. Kiki's all I have. Menaka doesn't even like her.'

He grabs me by the shirt, and with the help of two gym instructors, pulls me to my feet and pins me against the mirrored wall, making plaster sprinkle on my head.

'Menaka loves the kid,' he says. 'You have no bloody right to come in here and claim that she doesn't.'

'If this is about money –'

'That old bastard abandoned her once before and now he's trying to do it again. Menaka has to fight for what's hers. The money and the kid.'

'The kid has a name,' I say.

He slaps me. The punk slaps me with the front and the back of his hand.

'I'll give you all the money. Everything.'

Gayan leans away from me, eyebrows raised. 'That wouldn't work, but –'

'Just talk Menaka out of fighting for Kiki.'

Gayan looks down, mumbling to himself. He grabs me by the shirt, again, and, as if he has just remembered his lines, says, 'We love the kid. Both of us love that damn kid.'

'Bullshit.' I lunge at him, but the gym instructors pull me off. One raises a forty-five pound weight above my head.

I cry. In public. In a Rocky hard-man, wise-guy gym, I cry. I'm losing the plot.

Gayan spits on me and opens the gym door. 'Get out.'

I can't fight back the tears; covering my eyes, I limp down the steps.

I'm losing it, for sure.

I have seen Kiki for no more than half an hour today.

I drive home and find Kiki on Uncle Thilak's bed doing a puzzle; he's smiling blankly at her.

I go to her room and start packing her bags. I think I have to take her out of the country tonight, before they notice. Before they can grab her.

I bathe and dress her. Four years she's been mine alone and that bitch wants to take her. Kiki will be losing Uncle Thilak and me at the same time.

I dress her. Four years, I've been there every morning she's woken up bar one.

'Say goodbye to Seeya,' I say. 'We're going on holiday.'

She shakes her head. 'Seeya is sick, Daddy.'

'Yes, but he wants us to go. I promise you, he wants us to go.'

When I lift her, she screams the house down. Kicks out her legs till I release her.

'Seeya is sick, Dada. How can we go?'

I know she's right.

Every thought goes through my mind. I think of alternatives I think of approaching someone to bump Menaka off. I seriously consider it. Seriously, seriously.

Gayan – a bullet to that smug bloody face of his. A knife across his zig-zagged beard.

I take some Xanax and lie on the floor by Uncle Thilak's bed. Kiki is asleep next to him.

twenty-four

Uncle Thilak has his days when he's responsive. On other days, like today, he does not converse at all. He is sitting in his rocking chair on our terrace, overlooking the construction site of a housing complex. He lifts a hand to his mouth every few minutes as if taking his pills. But his hand is empty.

It is at times like this that I can sit with him, tell him my problems, cry on his shoulder. He doesn't call me a white little girl; he doesn't say anything.

The doctors say he's virtually comatose, but I think he hears me.

His eyes are blank. They have no life. Yet, they are fixed on Kiki's tree house. He blinks from time to time, but not often enough. His breaths are long and smooth, like the sounds of a calm sea. This is his peace, spoilt only by my moaning.

I ask him questions and then answer for him, like I used to do for Kiki before she learnt her first words.

'What should I do?' I ask him. 'How can I keep my baby?'

'Do whatever you need to,' I answer for him. 'You have my blessing.'

Then he looks at me. For once, he looks at me, and says, 'Kiki.' He holds his hands by his side, open-palmed. 'Kiki?'

'She's at nursery,' I say. 'She'll be home soon.'

'Kiki, Kiki,' he says.

'Menaka wants to take her for a day,' I say. 'Should I let her?'

'Kiki.' He holds his arms out as if to hug her.

'I can send one of your nurses with them, to feed her, keep her clean, you know?'

'Kiki.'

'Caroline said if they take her, they may realise it's too much for them. But what if Kiki likes them?'

He leans his head to one side. 'Kiki?'

'But Caroline says I can't stop them from taking her. That's like kidnapping, and for now they have asked only to take her on Saturdays. But what will we do on Saturdays without Kiki?'

'Kiki.' He smiles and closes his eyes.

'Saturdays. I'll dread Saturdays.'

Uncle Thilak, his eyes still shut, reaches a hand out towards me. I assume I am meant to hold it, so I do.

'Daddy,' he says. 'Daddy.'

It's Saturday. I'm on edge because I haven't slept at all; I'm surviving on Red Bull and coffee. Menaka and Gayan are coming to take my baby away from me in fifteen minutes. It's only for five hours. One hour more than she spends at nursery.

I can survive it. I think.

Uncle Thilak is in his non-responsive mode, but his breathing is different today, like a choppy ocean – short bursts with little gaps between them, the breaths all in different lengths.

Caroline knows I'm not coping too well, so she comes to see us. She packs Kiki's bag, while I explain to the nurse what she needs to do:

'Don't trust them to do anything themselves. Carry her if you cross roads. Keep her feet and legs covered at all times. Reapply mosquito lotion after four hours. Make sure she drinks water every hour. Give her strawberries after lunch. Make sure you wipe her hands if she touches the floor. Or any toys. Or other kids. Wipe her hands if Gayan touches them. Call me if she looks sick. Have a good time.'

'You sound like Uncle Thilak,' Caroline says.

Oh sweet Jesus.

✦

Menaka sends her driver. She doesn't even come herself to pick up my daughter. *Her* daughter. This is the pits, but I take note of this in case I have to fight her in court.

I try to call Menaka to abuse her but Caroline takes the phone out of my hand.

'Don't give them anything to give their lawyers. If you have custody of Kiki –'

'If?'

'*When* you get official custody of Kiki, you're going to have to give Menaka the chance to see her. You know that, right? So you have to show you can.'

It's probably a good thing Caroline and I have not 'started partaking in the jiggy-jiggy bang-bang', as Uncle Thilak says. Because we're not attached in that way, she can see this as an outsider and as a friend.

'Great that the driver's here for her. Less time with the bitch,' she says.

I like that she calls Menaka a bitch with such passion.

'Send both nurses with her,' she says. 'We'll look after the old man.'

Kiki cries when she is put in the car. I can never say it is a good thing to see your daughter cry, but that is how I feel now. She knows who she is going to see and she's not happy. This makes me feel good in a sick I'm-a-bastard-kind-of-way.

Caroline and I try to have lunch but when I serve it, I see Kiki's little Crocs by the table. Those tiny shoes, for those tiny feet I love so much. It's been the worst half hour of my life.

I can't eat. Even smoking is too hard. I pace up and down the garden. Caroline rocks in a chair, trying to look calm but I can tell she's not.

The garden is littered with Kiki's things. Her trampoline, her wheelbarrow and bike, her tree house and skates. Her inflated swimming pool.

Will they bring her back?

This is too much for me.

I take out my phone to call Menaka to beg her to bring Kiki home but I have to hang up before she answers because Ranjith is shouting from upstairs. His voice is high-pitched. Frantic.

'Master, master.'

I leap up the stairs, overtaking Caroline.

Uncle Thilak lies naked, sprawled across his bedroom floor. He has a cut on his forehead and is peeing on himself, on his tummy and up to his chest, up to his feeding tube.

Ranjith shouts something in Sinhala I cannot understand and I don't want to. His job was to watch Uncle Thilak for a moment, so how the hell the old man ended up naked on the floor I don't know. Caroline is about to enter the room but I wave her away. Uncle Thilak wouldn't want her to see him like this.

She wouldn't want to see him like this.

I kneel down next to him, sliding in his pee. I rub him down with a towel. He is crying. I haven't seen that from him in this state. I didn't think he felt pain or emotion.

'Kiki,' he says.

'Call Menaka, babe,' I say. 'Tell her I think Uncle Thilak needs Kiki. She needs to bring her home.'

Even before Caroline called, Kiki was on her way home with Menaka's driver. Gayan and Menaka lasted only half an hour with her. According to the nurses, Kiki whined all the time she was there, begging to go home. Good girl.

Back home, she tries to get into Uncle Thilak's room but I have to clean and dress him first. Once that's done, I unlock the door and Caroline tries to pass Kiki to me, but I can't take her. I've cleaned the old man but I haven't had a chance to clean myself.

Kiki jumps on the bed next to Uncle Thilak. He passes her a book. *Baby's First Words*, it's called.

Kiki is far past that. Pointing to a picture of a duck, she asks, 'What does the duck say?'

Smiling, Uncle Thilak says, 'Quack quack.' Then he turns the page. 'Dog says woof woof.'

twenty-five

Menaka asks to meet me. She says she wants to settle on an outcome which we are all happy with, an outcome that will benefit Kiki the most.

I wonder if she wants to talk cash. I hope so. She can have it all, if she signs something saying she wants me to have custody of Kiki.

✧

I pause outside Eroshan's Shell, a drinking establishment on the beach. The empty bar looks like a stage. A kerosene lamp hangs from each of the four wooden pillars that hold up the roof. A piece of straw falls into one of the lamps' flames, which makes it brighter for a split second. Menaka is already there, and behind her a backdrop so faultless it looks like a theatre set itself; the Indian Ocean reflects the full moon, with a smudge of yellow following it to shore. Menaka's hair is in her face; maybe the sea breeze blew it there, maybe she is trying to hide the tears that roll down her cheeks.

She doesn't stand for me and I don't reach for her.

Shaking sea shells on her palms, she digs her toes into the sand.

I point to the bottle on the table. The remaining arrack is just above the halfway mark of a small bottle. 'Please don't tell me you've drunk that on your own.'

She pats the plastic seat next to her. When I sit, the legs dig into the sand and my chin is barely above the table.

She leans over to hug me. I neither welcome her hug nor deflect it. My arms remain by my side while hers drape my upper back. She buries her head in the gap between my shoulder and neck, her weeping concealed by the slapping of the waves against the beach.

I don't ask questions. I wait.

Five minutes. Maybe more.

Leaning out of the hug, her eyes are black, eyeliner dripping down her face. She looks unattractive, for possibly the first time in her life.

I see a bruise just below her collarbone, but am not sure if it is a shadow. It looks purple, but so does the sea beyond us.

'I want to leave Gayan,' she says.

This is good news. I hope I don't show my excitement.

'He wants too much. More than I can give.'

'I'm sorry to hear that.' I clutch her hands.

She closes her eyes. 'I told him and he didn't take it well.'

The bruises?

'It's understandable though. I promised him a lot, but again I can't deliver.'

The one question I want to ask, the one question I care about, concerns Kiki. Would she fight for her still?

'It's me,' she says. 'I know that. It's me.'

'Your father told me about abandoning you.'

She reclines in the chair, brushes her hair out of her eyes and wipes her cheeks with the back of her hand. 'He told you?'

I nod. I don't feel the need to make it clear that Aiya told me. It's enough, I think, that Uncle Thilak tried to.

'That's an odd relationship you've got there. He's never told me anything personal.'

'He denies it now. Must have been the drugs.'

'I guess.' She tries to make eye contact but turns away. 'Did he feel bad about it?'

'Very.'

'Thank you for looking after him,' she says. 'The white man subservient to him. He must love that.'

'Barely acknowledges me. It's all about Kiki.'

'Maybe, but he'd turn his back on her the second she did something he didn't like.'

'He's changed, I think.'

Menaka mocks a laugh. 'You're defending him? After all he did to you?'

'I'm telling you, he regrets what happened.'

'Then why is he leaving all the money meant for me to Kiki?' She starts crying again. 'Why, if he feels so bad about abandoning me, is he abandoning me again?'

I don't really know how to answer this. 'How do you know? How do you know he's not leaving you anything?'

'He told me. We had a fight and he told me. Unless you know differently?'

'Not a clue.'

Menaka looks at her flashing phone. 'Forty-six missed calls from Gayan.'

'Don't answer,' I say.

'I wonder, sometimes, what would happen if you and I got back together.' She turns the phone face-down. 'Lived together in the house we built. With the daughter we created.'

I hold my breath; I can't say anything. I can't say that I'm interested. As much as I think I love Caroline, getting back with Menaka is tempting, if it means I won't lose Kiki. I've thought about this often enough. I don't think anyone knows what true love is until they have children.

'But you have that blonde girl now, no?' she asks.

I sense that as long as I pretend I am with Caroline, Menaka will want to be with me. As soon as Menaka gets me, she will lose interest.

'Yes,' I say.

'You sound unsure.'

'We're not rushing into anything.'

Menaka ambles onto the beach proper and sits down, cross-legged. 'Kiki likes her?'

I slump onto the sand. 'Loves her.'

'She calls her Mummy?'

'No, no.' I have to lie. The moment demands it. 'Caroline wouldn't allow that.'

The reflection of the moon spreads across the ocean like spilt paint and lights up Menaka's smile. 'Caroline. What a generic name. What a safe, boring name.'

'She's far from boring.'

Lying down on the sand, Menaka rests her head on my lap. I look around to see if anyone can see this. I assume, for a second, that this would displease Caroline, but maybe that is arrogant of me. Maybe Caroline thinks of herself as just a friend of mine. Maybe she really does want to work things out with Sujeewa, get back with him. So I stroke Menaka's hair and I start imagining where we could end up tonight. I have to nudge her head to the side of my legs so that she doesn't feel this imagination of mine.

We stay like this for a few minutes. Silent. She slides onto her knees and looks at me.

A stray dog barks, approaches us, wants attention, but not as much as Menaka.

Menaka, a woman I have spent the last couple of months

hating. When she talked about taking my daughter from me, I wanted to destroy her.

But now, with the moon over her shoulder, the waves between her legs, she is everything I knew. The beauty, the shine of her skin, the flow of her hair. The softness of her hands against my cheeks. Her eyes, free from her green contact lenses, cartoon large. Her lips on mine. Her breath. Her tongue.

～✺

She wakes in my bed, but doesn't speak. I ask her questions but she just cries. I try to cuddle her but she pushes me away and wraps the sheet around her naked body.

'Please,' she says. 'Just leave me alone for a few moments.'

I check on Kiki. I check on Uncle Thilak. Both are asleep. Both are breathing.

I come back to the room and Menaka is in her own clothes. 'You never emptied my closet?'

'Too lazy,' I say.

'Or you wanted me back.' Menaka tip-toes towards Kiki's room and opens her door. 'I think this is what I want,' she says. 'I think I'm ready.'

Reaching a hand out to mine, she strokes her finger across my palm. 'I think I'm ready.'

I try to make eye contact but she is looking down at her feet. I want to tell her that I am not sure. I love Caroline. So does Kiki. You've missed your chance. I don't love you anymore.

But after what happened last night, I don't have the balls to say all this. And I don't have the balls to risk her wrath if that means she will try to take Kiki from me.

So, even after she has kissed me on the cheeks and left the house, I feel trapped. Boxed in. I can't go one way or the other and it makes me collapse on the floor.

Until I hear Kiki calling me from her bed.

I go to see her. And I hug her. And I know that I can't do it to Kiki. I can't bring Menaka back into her life because I know she will go. I know she will leave us.

The thing is, I want her to leave us.

Kiki is on the trampoline. Caroline is here now and it worries me how normal I am with her. As if I have done nothing wrong. Maybe I haven't. We're just friends. Menaka is still my wife.

Do I need to tell her anything?

Do I need to come clean?

'You look tired,' she says.

'I've a lot on my mind.'

'Share.'

I watch Kiki and rub my eyes. 'Jump higher,' I say. I have to be honest with Caroline. I know I do. 'There's something you're not telling me, isn't there?' I ask.

'Am I that transparent?'

'You've seen Sujeewa, haven't you?'

'Last Friday. I went to see him, to tell him it's over.'

'The break?'

'The relationship,' she says.

I straighten my back. The pressure is on. 'But you still need space?'

'I don't think so.'

I ruffle up my hair. Bugger, bugger, bugger. Bad timing. 'You mean?'

'I can't think about starting anything with you until I'm completely honest,' she says. 'You're going to hate me.'

'I don't like the sound of this.'

'I felt sorry for Sujeewa.' She wipes a tear off her cheek. 'I kept saying no to everything he asked.'

'Like?'

'Can we have one more try? One more month to fix things? A trip away to clear the air.'

I thought about my break-ups. What I would then ask for. 'He asked for break-up sex?'

'I said no, but we hugged and...'

'Did it mean anything?'

'Of course not.' Her sobbing makes her hiccup. 'We've broken up. I may never see him again.'

'Except on TV.' This bothered me because I thought his high profile would make it harder for her to forget him.

She tries to smile. 'Not if we don't watch cricket.'

I rock my body back and forth. I expect to be more upset, but maybe I am used to the idea of her sleeping with him. Maybe I thought she always was.

'It meant nothing to me. I just felt...'

I start crying. I just can't hold it back. This is the opportunity to come clean. 'I have something to tell you too.'

'I feared this,' she says. 'Plan B?'

'There was no plan B,' I say. 'But I met Menaka last night.'

'I know. She got my number and texted me.' Caroline rubs her eyes. 'Just answer one question,' she says. 'Would you ever get back with her?'

'Not a hope in hell.'

Caroline hugs me, and takes stuttering breaths.

We don't talk. Don't kiss. Just hold each other.

twenty-six

I tell Caroline the full details of my night with Menaka. It's important we start a relationship with the truth, with nothing to hide.

This is the sort of man I have become. Upfront, morally excellent.

Besides, I know Menaka will tell her anyway.

Caroline pretends to take it well but there is new venom in her hatred for Menaka, and new passion in her love for Kiki.

Menaka is still pissed off that I rejected her. I get at least one text a day from her, informing me about her pending legal action, telling me to get ready to lose Kiki.

Each message hurts, but less than the one before.

Uncle Thilak drifts in and out of awareness. When Kiki has her afternoon nap, I spend those two hours in his room. Sometimes he recognises me, sometimes he doesn't. Sometimes, even if he does recognise me, he has nothing to say.

At other times, like today, he is chatty. I take him for a drive past the paddy fields and lakes.

'Where is the blondie?' he asks.

'She's at work.'

'Where does she work?'

I've told him about sixty times. 'At the school. She's a teacher.'

'Ah, a teacher. And what does she do for a living?'

'She's a teacher,' I say.

'Ah, that's nice. My daughter is a teacher, no?'

I don't see any point in correcting him because he's likely pulling my leg. 'That's right.'

'Is Caroline a teacher?'

Ugh. He's winding me up for sure.

He turns around to look in the back seat. 'Where's Kiki?'

'Sleeping, uncle, like I told you. We'll talk to her when she wakes up.'

'If anything happens to you, I can look after her,' he says.

'Thank you, uncle.'

'I'm very good with kids.'

'Yes, you are, uncle.'

'I'm a very capable man.'

'You are.'

'I can look after myself.'

'You're a big boy.'

'Now tell me...' He signals for me to slow down. 'Are you going to marry the blondie?'

'I don't know.' I always get the feeling he is more lucid than he lets on.

'She's a teacher.'

'That's right.'

'And white. You're white.'

'Keeping the bloodline strong.'

'Yes, but Kiki is brown. She's going to look like she was adopted.'

I press down on the accelerator again and drive faster than I should. 'She looks like me.'

Uncle Thilak laughs, which makes him cough and clutch his mouth. 'Oh dear *suddha*. That little girl looks like an angel. You look like bird shit.'

'Charming.'

'My favourite joke,' he says. 'What do you do if a bird shits on your windscreen?'

'Don't know.'

'You break up with her,' he says. 'You break up with her.'

The joke is still funny, even though he's told it to me thousands of times.

'Don't repeat this.' Uncle Thilak cups a hand around his mouth. 'I'm getting old and I may not be around forever.'

'What an enormous pity,' I say. 'I'll miss your charm.'

'You must look after that girl. Kiki. She is special. Very, very special.'

'I'll never do anything but look after her.'

'She has a great deal of potential. She could become a doctor, a lawyer, a president.'

'Kiki's four years old.'

'So is Shahid Afridi.'

I chuckle. 'I think they say he's five now.'

'Just keep her happy, okay. Make sure she feels loved. Don't let my daughter take her.'

'There's not a hope in hell I will,' I say.

'Okay, good. Now I just shat my pants, so please take me home.'

Every day I wake up dreading the worst; that I may get news that Menaka has opened up proceedings to win custody of Kiki. But in some ways I want it. I just want to have it out there so that I can confront it. I have to confront it and I can't until Menaka makes the first move.

So when Priyanga, my lawyer, tells me that her counsel has been in touch with him, I feel relieved. I just want to be able to discuss every option available to me.

Caroline is with Kiki and Uncle Thilak, so it's as good a time to visit Priyanga as any, especially since it's bloody hard to find a time when he's actually awake.

I go to Uncle Thilak's room. Caroline is asleep on the sofa and Uncle Thilak is in the wheelchair, with Kiki on his lap. He is kissing her head, but appears as engrossed in *Dora the Explorer* as she is. I say bye to both of them, but neither take their eyes off the TV. Kiki has both her little hands on Uncle Thilak's wrists.

At four years of age, her forearms are thicker than his.

Priyanga seems to be in a different world when I enter his office. In fact, if I am to guess, I would say he's focusing on his breathing and posture as he nibbles his pumpkin seeds.

His office is a round table on an open veranda amongst palm trees.

'Ah,' he says. 'Mr Johnson, your prostitute has indeed filed a case against you.'

I hold up my hand. 'Wait, wait, I'm Mr Trusted.'

Priyanga taps his desk. 'So you are. Um, do you know Mr Peter Johnson, from Maitland Crescent?'

'I do, yes.'

'Well, could I please ask you to disregard what I just said then? My apologies. You're here about...' He fiddles around with the files on his desk.

'My divorce to Menaka Rupasinghe. You phoned me about an hour ago.'

'Ah yes, so I did, Mr Johnson.'

'Mr Trusted.'

'Sit, sit.' He points to the side of the table that doesn't have space for a chair, so I go the opposite way. 'Divorce here is fault-based, which means your wife had to come up with a reason for divorcing you. She has claimed adultery.'

'What?' I stand up and walk over to see the papers he is looking at, but he signals for me to return to my seat. 'That's outrageous.'

'Well, the other options were malicious desertion or impotency. She has to find a fault, you see.'

'But she committed adultery, not me.'

'Um. You realise you're still married, correct?'

'Yes, of course,' I say.

'Well, have you begun a relationship with anyone else?'

'Only after she did.'

'So she is in a relationship?' he asks.

'Not anymore, I don't think.'

'But you are?'

'Yes, but it's only been for –'

'You are?'

I nod.

'Okay, so we could try to argue that you assumed separation, or that you felt she abandoned you. You've had no, how should we say, intimate relations since she left back in 2011?'

'With Menaka? Do you mean regularly?' I ask.

'I mean at all, and I am your lawyer so you shouldn't waste my time by lying.'

'Once.'

'When was this?'

'A few weeks ago, but –'

'A few weeks ago.' He writes that down and once finished, looks up at me. 'She has claimed she wanted to resurrect the relationship. That you led her to believe that you wanted that too, but then you cheated on her.'

'That's not how it happened,' I say.

'Can you dispute that claim in a practical sense?'

'Why is all of this relevant? Can I just accept the divorce and move on?'

He smiles. 'I think that's what she wants, but bear in mind she will win a battle for alimony and she will win custody. Here the law treats women as being capable of little more than bringing up children. They won't deem her able to earn money for herself, so you will have to support her and her child.'

'My child.'

'Your child?' he asks.

'She's my child too.'

'Oh yes, of course, Mr Johnson. Sorry, I was thinking you were someone else for a moment. Anyway, the courts will see it as her child.'

'Her name is Kiki.'

'The court will see it as Kiki's child.'

'No, no, Kiki is my daughter,' I say.

Priyanga slams his file shut and rests his elbows on top of it. 'I'll not waste your time. I would not advise you to contest this.'

'But what if they ask Kiki where she wants to live?'

He opens his file again and perches his glasses on the end of his nose. 'She's four years old?'

'That's right.'

'No, that won't do anything for you. Mr Johnson –'

'Trusted.'

'Mr Trusted, it is my opinion that you must try to settle this outside of the legal system.'

'How would you suggest I do that?'

'Um. Thilak Rupasinghe was my mentor. A great man. He called me a few months before you did the first time and asked me to help you, so I can assume he's on your side.'

'He thinks I'd make the better parent.'

'Ask him to buy your wife out.' Priyanga takes a deep breath. 'If what you said on the phone is right, and that all your wife wants is access to your daughter's inheritance, then ask him to buy her out.'

'I don't think he's communicative enough for that now.'

Standing, Priyanga directs me to his door. 'This is your only reasonable option. If you don't want to lose your daughter, you need Mr Rupasinghe to broker a deal.'

'If that fails?'

'Well, of course I wouldn't suggest that you should try to sneak your daughter out of the country as that would be against the law. Even if it was your only reasonable option in a bid to keep your daughter with the parent she loves.' He picks up the phone, upside down at first. 'Now if you'll excuse me, I have someone waiting.' He speaks into the phone. 'Please, can you send Mr Trusted in?'

Caroline agrees to stay with my two dependents while I drive around, gathering my thoughts. In normal circumstances, I can get lost in the scenery: the paddy fields on either side of the road, the birds, the water. But today, I think. I need to be smart.

Priyanga is a genius disguised as an utter fool. He uncovered how perfectly Menaka has played me. She is always on top, always in control. Although he didn't say as much, Priyanga may have realised that her break-up with Gayan was faked too. If it wasn't that, it was always her intention to use him. It is too much of a coincidence that she asked me to get back together with her just as I found Caroline, just as Caroline broke up with her boyfriend for good. Menaka would have known that. She knows everything about everyone in Colombo.

So in the eyes of the court, even though she abandoned her child, she will now look like the victim. She tried to get back with me and I said yes, but now I have shunned her.

I would not have had much of a chance in court anyway, but this just seals it.

I have to pack my bags and get Kiki out of the country.

We're on the swing under the sprawling vines of the banyan tree.

'I understand,' Caroline says. 'I do. You must feel desperate, but if you're caught –'

'I won't be caught,' I say. 'I can't be.'

'They'll take her from you... You'll lose any chance of winning custody.'

'I need you to back me up. Cover for me. Please, baba.'

'I'll look after Uncle Thilak,' she says. 'But I'm not around forever.'

'If they ask you if you knew of my plans, you have to say no.'

'Or I'm in the shit, too?' Caroline winks. 'Yeah, I'll keep my mouth shut about that one.'

'Why don't you just come with us?'

'You know why,' she says.

'But he's not your responsibility,' I say, guilt kicking me in the guts.

'Just go.'

'When will we –'

'Just go, go, go, go,' she says, tears down her cheeks, her eyes red. 'Please, just bloody go.'

Our bags are packed.

I knock on Uncle Thilak's door and Caroline opens it. Sweating. Panting.

Uncle Thilak is in his wheelchair, looking mischievous. Kiki runs and jumps into my arms, saying something I don't really catch.

'Uncle Thilak, Kiki and I need to go out for a moment or two,' I say.

'Kiki may need to go out,' he says. 'But it's about bloody time you came out.'

'Language,' Caroline says.

'English, woman,' Uncle Thilak says. 'English.'

'He's been like this for the last hour,' Caroline says. 'Extra pain relief was needed.'

'Can you manage?' I ask.

'Just about.' She slaps his hand away from her arse. 'But he's getting a little frisky.'

I lean over Uncle Thilak. This is the last time I will ever see him and I know it. I think he does too. He knows. Somehow, he always knows.

I kiss him on his head. Not a single hair on it.

'Kiki,' he says, 'I told you your father fancies me.'

'Ignore him, darling,' I say. 'Kiss him goodbye.'

She crosses her arms and tucks her chin in. 'No, I will not. He's very mean today.'

'I didn't let the little princess take my wheelchair,' he says. 'Time you grow up, little girl. You're no baby anymore.'

'Kiss him, please,' I say.

'Just leave it, jackass,' he says. 'Leave me alone. Get out, all of you.'

I kiss him on the head again.

Caroline is rubbing her eyes. I lift Kiki onto my shoulders so that she is looking behind me, but I think she can feel that I'm crying.

twenty-seven

The airport is as brightly lit as a photographer's studio, its vast expanse of white floors and walls exposing me like a prisoner in no-man's land.

The porters in fluorescent yellow vests, leaning against their lop-sided trolleys; the army commanders in combat gear, their fingers on triggers even though the war is over; the air force officers in blue, manning the X-ray machines, pointing at Kiki, giggling and sticking their tongues out; the passengers, all judging me, whispering to each other about my baby girl. Yes, I know she's got tears in her eyes, you twats.

I'm hiding under an oversized New York Yankees baseball cap. But they recognise me. They know me as the white man who married into the Rupasinghe family. They recognise my chin and my nose even if they can't see my eyes.

I queue for the Colombo to London flight. It's the first time I've had to queue for anything since I married Menaka. This is the only flight left tonight. There are four queues and no hurry, but everyone is bunched too close to me. I can feel a trolley against my calf and the hairy arm of a passenger against my hand.

Over-burdened by the forty pounds of sleeping child in my arms, my biceps pumped with blood, I squat, resting Kiki on my knees.

A woman in uniform sari taps my shoulder and nudges me towards the front of the queue. 'Where are your bags?'

I look down at the flip-flops I am wearing, Uncle Thilak's. Much too small for me, so more flop than flip. 'I left them in the taxi.'

'The baby's things?'

No toys, milk, snacks, books or boiled water. 'I'll buy some from the departure lounge.'

'Sir, you won't find anything through there. On the flight they'll give what they have for kids but that's not much.' She turns her back to the check-in desk and cups her hand against my ear. 'You can't fly like this. Let me book you on tomorrow's flight and you can get everything together and come back.'

'I'm going tonight.'

Kiki rubs her eyes and moans at the queue for immigration. She wants to go home to her Seeya. She wants to say goodbye, but I beg her to be quiet for a few hours. I lie and tell her we're going away for just a week. I'll buy her something big from the shops upstairs, I say. She sucks in deep breaths and accepts my bribe.

'She's hungry,' a pug-faced woman filling in an embarkation card says.

'No shit,' I say. It pisses me off that people always tell me things about my child, as if I wouldn't know because I'm a man.

It's my turn at the counter so I pop a Lorazepam pill.

The immigration officer has black hair, but his eyebrows and beard are white. His name tag says Perera. I wonder if he's related to the three hundred other Pereras I've met in my five years in Colombo.

Perera smiles at Kiki and holds a pen out to her.

'She's hungry?'

I try to force a smile. 'Yes, very long journey to the airport.'

'She's sleepy too.' He looks back down at his open palm. 'Passports please?'

I fish our documents out of the back pocket of my jeans.

Perera opens up the door to his booth and invites Kiki in.

Against my better judgement I let her go. He puts her on his lap and lets her play with his computer mouse. He swipes and stamps my British passport and returns it, but then yanks it back out of my grip. 'Edward Trusted, this is your child, no?'

'Of course,' I say.

'But her surname is Rupasinghe.'

I bow over the counter. 'My father-in-law wanted that. It should be Rupasinghe-Trusted.'

'But it just says Rupasinghe.'

'Yes.'

'Do you have her birth certificate with you?' he asks.

'Why would I need that?'

'Because it would say who Kiki's father is.'

'I am.' Kiki comes out of the booth and taps my waist, wanting me to pick her up.

'I have no proof of that,' Perera says. 'Who has the birth certificate?'

'My father-in-law, I would think.'

Perera rubs his forehead and clicks the mouse on his computer. 'Do you have a letter from your wife saying you can travel alone with the child?'

'Surely that's not required, is it?'

'Have you travelled alone with her before?'

'Not abroad, no.'

'What to do?' He asks. 'Can't let you leave without consent from her mother. Please check again, in your pocket, if you have a letter of consent from your wife.'

'I know I don't.'

'Can see one.' He points to the pocket with my wallet in it and hands me back my passport. 'Put it in here and return it.'

I get what he wants but I have no idea how much to give. I chance it and slip a hundred dollar bill into my passport and hand it back to him.

He looks at it like a poker player checking his hand.

'Will that do?' I ask.

He doesn't look up. 'Yes, but I will need five copies of it.'

I slide four more hundred dollar bills over the counter and he stamps both our passports.

'Have a pleasant flight, with that lovely daughter of yours. She looks just like you, you know?'

I flash Uncle Thilak's credit card at the entrance to the Araliya Lounge and chase after Kiki as she struts towards the buffet counter. It wouldn't be Sri Lanka if I didn't see someone Kiki's related to. Gayan's father, Gehan Rupasinghe, is on the far side of the lounge, legs up on a leather couch.

I stand with my back to him, blocking Kiki as I nudge her towards the bathrooms.

The swing doors of the ladies' room open, almost knocking Kiki over.

'Kiki,' a woman says. 'Eddie, is that you?'

I recognise Thilini Rupasinghe's fake accent straightaway.

I say, 'Sorry, I'm in a bit of a rush.'

Thilini points towards Kiki. 'Accident?'

'Something like that,' I say, even though it's insulting since Kiki is four (or *fow*, as Thilini would say).

'My husband's outside.' Thilini says.

'Yes, I saw him, but he seemed busy. Look, shall I come speak to you guys when I'm done?'

'You don't want any help?' she asks.

'It's not like you can come into the gents. When I'm done maybe you can play with her. You know how she loves playing with you.'

Thilini intertwines her arms together, bows her head, lifts her gaze. 'I am her favourite aunty. Okay, see you outside. Where are you going by the way?'

'Please, I'll talk when I come out.' I put a hand on her shoulder. 'Look, don't tell anyone you saw us here.'

'Why not?' she asks. 'A little surprise for Menaka?'

'Something like that.'

'Or a little surprise for some other lady?'

The noisy bitch. Ugh. I can't trust her. I know that, so I have to pull out the big guns. 'If anyone finds out I'm here, I'd hate to have to release the list of beautiful ladies who procure the services of off-duty cops for sex.'

Thilini shrugs her shoulder and giggles. 'What are you talking about?'

'You know what I mean.'

Silence. Her lips quiver, but she says nothing, stumbling back and propping herself up against the wall.

'Understood?' I ask.

She nods.

❦

We clear security and settle down right next to the departure gates. Kiki is playing some game with herself that I don't understand. My feet tap in time with the movement of the seconds' hand of the clock. The clock's moving too slow. I have more nervous energy to burn than that.

Kiki slumps next to me, but won't communicate. Her feet are

on the seats, which I would tell her off about normally, but this is not the time.

The announcement to board.

I'm so close to being away, so close to keeping Kiki, but I certainly don't want to celebrate too early. The Rupasinghes can crush dreams in a second. That plane just needs to take off. Then we're away.

I am more confident when I put Kiki down so that her feet touch the floor of the plane. Yet, we're chased by heavy footsteps, getting louder, getting closer, past the air-bridge, onto the plane.

A man, dressed in a black suit and tie, squeezes his way past queuing passengers. I turn my back on him but he leans around my body to look at my face.

'Edward Trusted?'

I ignore the question, instead tending to the apparent needs of a grumpy child.

The man puts a hand on my shoulder.

'What the hell do you want?' I ask.

Backing away, his hands up by his face, he says, 'You left your passports, sir. When I checked your boarding cards, you left before I could give your passports back.'

I bow my head and close my eyes. 'I'm so sorry. I'm so so sorry. It's been a tough day.'

I bend the passports into my back pocket and sit down to make Kiki wear her seatbelt, even though she is slapping her arms and legs around to stop me. 'Be quiet and sit still,' I say.

'Sir,' the flight attendant says, her hand on the back of the chair.

'What?' I say. 'She'll be quiet if you guys just leave us be.'

'You have to put your seat up, sir, and lift your window shade for take-off.'

'Haven't you got more important things to do?' I labour to do as told to make the point that travelling with a child is hard enough without the crew being pedantic.

'Cabin crew prepare for take-off.'

A flight attendant leans back and heaves the door closed, before sitting down and strapping herself into her seat.

The engines rumble, the plane jerks into reverse.

Oh my god. Could this be working? Can I get to England and not have to worry about Menaka stealing Kiki from me?

I look out the window at the palm trees. At the rubber trees. At Sri Lanka.

The best country in the world.

My home.

Kiki's home.

Uncle Thilak's home.

Uncle Thilak, who we will never see again.

The terminal is further away. Smaller. It's happening.

I have to text Caroline. It's the last chance.

'Please try to explain to Uncle Thilak. Sometimes he understands. Tell him Kiki loves him and is so angry with me for not letting her stay with him. Thank him from me for looking after my baby. Tell him I'm sorry I couldn't say goodbye. I hope he doesn't suffer too much. I love you. Please forgive me and come to London soon.'

I press send just before the flight attendant tells me off for having my phone on.

A toddler to the left of us starts crying, which sets Kiki off, almost as if in competition to see if she can be louder. She is not as proficient at fake-crying as her mother.

'You're too old for this,' I say. 'Rupasinghes don't cry.'

I undo my seatbelt and stand in the aisle, Kiki in my arms fighting to get out.

'Sit down, sir,' the flight attendant says.

'Just give me a minute or two, please.'

The flight attendant undoes her seatbelt and marches towards me, grabbing my shoulder. 'Sir, we cannot take off until you sit down.'

'Okay, okay,' I say. 'Your bloody fault now if she cries all the way to London.'

I can feel people staring at me. 'Quiet,' I say again to Kiki. 'You need to be quiet.'

'I want to go home.'

My phones pings. Shit, I haven't put it off. Filthy look from the cabin crew but I read the message anyway.

From Caroline.

'I don't think Uncle Thilak will make it through the night. He's asking for Kiki. The doctors are here, but they say there's no point in moving him. Just have to make him comfortable. I think I better not tell him Kiki's left.'

'Put your phone off, sir.'

I start typing out a text.

'Sir, put your phone off and sit down or we will have to stop the plane and have you removed.'

'We should have him removed anyway,' a passenger says.

I read my text back to myself. Think. Think. Think.

I look at my watch and send the message: 'Just tell him that Kiki will be back home to see him in an hour and a half. Tell him to hold on.'

twenty-eight

We're on our way home in a van owned by a man whose driving suggests he wants to beat Uncle Thilak to the grave. This suits me, as I have to get far away before I have to bribe any more security officials after the fracas I caused on the plane.

Kiki is asleep on my lap. I am normally anal about her using a child seat, but in this instance we didn't have time to source a taxi with one. I am strapped in myself, and I hold onto Kiki with all my strength, except when I am on the phone to Caroline. She tells me that Uncle Thilak is as lucid as he has been for a long time. He's as aware of his surrounding as one could hope from a man who knows he is about to die.

Menaka is in town but Aiya is in Sydney. I call him, waking him up in the middle of the night there, telling him what is happening. He says he'll be on the next flight and that he will call his sister. I can't bear the thought of seeing Menaka but I know that Uncle Thilak will want to say goodbye to his daughter. Of course he would.

I am pleased that, by the time we arrive home, Menaka is not there. I wonder if we can say goodbye to Uncle Thilak and then run off again. Vanish.

Caroline is standing on the landing outside Uncle Thilak's room. 'I think you have to be quick.'

We inch up the stairs, Kiki insisting that I can't carry her.

Uncle Thilak's eyes are three quarters shut. He doesn't look a great deal different to how he did when we left, except that he smiles when Kiki calls out his name.

I help her up onto his bed and she rests her head on his chest. There is always the chance that she will become too playful and hyperactive, but so far she's gold.

I don't think he has the strength to lift his own arm up, but when I see his fingers twitch, I do it for him. His hand is now on Kiki's back.

'I love you, Seeya,' Kiki says. 'Are you really leaving?'

'I have to, *chooti kella*.' He takes in a deep breath and closes his mouth, as if trapping a cough.

'Where are you going?'

'Somewhere from where I can always watch you and that jackass father of yours.'

'Yes, he's a silly bugger,' Kiki says.

'A white fool,' Uncle Thilak says.

I sniff, almost cry, but Caroline looks at me and I hold it in.

'Seeya,' Kiki says, 'will you write to me from where you are?'

'I'll try, my darling. Can you read?'

'I'm a big girl now.'

'Yes you are. Very big.'

Uncle Thilak turns to face me. 'I have left some things in my top drawer for Kiki. Make sure she gets them. Don't plunder them, you colonialist bastard.'

'Sure,' I say.

'Will I see my son and daughter?'

'Aiya has told Menaka. But he's in Sydney.'

'What the hell is he doing there?'

'He lives there,' I say.

'Idiot. My daughter won't come. Not high profile enough for her here.'

'She'll be here,' I say. 'She loves you.'

'Maybe,' Uncle Thilak says. He coughs and I can see blood on his teeth. '*Chooti kella*, you better go to bed now.'

'But, Seeya, I want to sleep here.'

'I have to leave now,' he says.

'No, Seeya, no.'

'And I have to say goodbye to your father.'

Caroline appears to have been instructed about what she needs to do. She kisses Kiki and lifts her off Seeya. Kiki is kicking her legs out.

Caroline hugs her. 'Give Seeya a nice kiss.'

Kiki stops complaining and kisses Uncle Thilak on the head. 'I love you, Seeya.'

Somehow lifting his hands for himself, Uncle Thilak holds her face. 'I love you more. Grow up to be a good girl. A strong girl.'

Cupping his hands around Kiki's ear, he says something no one but her can hear.

'Yes, Seeya,' Kiki says. 'Promise.'

'What did he say?' I ask.

'Mind your own business.' His eyes bulge as he coughs out more blood. 'Kiki, never tell anyone I said that.' He signals for me to take her out of the room.

'Menaka's here,' I say.

'Tell her to wait. I need to speak to you.'

Caroline takes Kiki from me. They stop at the door. Kiki, silent, tears pouring down her face, has one final look at her grandfather.

When the door closes I hear Menaka's voice, then Kiki cries. Menaka knocks on the door.

'Lock it, *suddha*.'

I do as told.

'Quick, quick,' he says.

I kneel down by his bed, which is low enough for me to rest my elbows on.

'*Suddha*, don't let Kiki wear make-up. Don't let her wear short skirts. Make sure you check the male friends she has. Don't let her drink till she's twenty-one.' He coughs more blood. 'Tell her to respect her elders. Don't let her spend time with male cousins. Tell her there is no need to commit to people if you are scared to commit. No rush to get married.'

He pauses and takes in three deep breaths.

'Tell her there's no need to try to prove herself. No one to try to battle. Just enjoy life. Tell her I loved her as much as I could possibly love anything and she made my life better than I could have hoped. That's it.'

'Shall I let Menaka in now?' I ask.

'Wait, you bugger. I have words for you too.'

'Have you got time?' I ask.

'Let me check my diary.'

'You know what I mean.'

I can tell he's trying to reach for my hand but it's a struggle so I lean in towards him.

'I wanted to tell you something.' He looks at his feet which pop out, below the sheet, at the end of the bed. 'Remember, at hospital that day when you got me drunk –'

'I got you drunk?'

'Very irresponsible.' He tries to smile. 'Well, there's been something that has haunted me for so long. Something I did that made Menaka who she is.'

I put my hand on his shoulder. 'Don't worry about it, Aiya told me.'

'Aiya?' he asks. 'Impossible. What did he say?'

'How you kicked Menaka out when she was sixteen because –'

'Oh that.' He grips my hand. 'No, no. That's no secret. Everyone knows that.'

'It can't be worse, can it?' I slap my forehead with the back of my hand, knowing I've been insensitive.

'Much worse. Unspeakably bad. And you know what?' He is crying, his eyes closing, missing breaths. 'I couldn't live with myself, but I couldn't die until I made amends.'

I am desperate to find out what this secret is, but I know this is killing him. 'You don't have to tell me.'

'I don't have to tell you, no, but I have to tell Menaka. I have to tell Aiya. They have to know.'

I put a hand to my chest. 'You want me to tell them?'

'Well done, Einstein.' He tries to give me the thumbs-up. 'You're a coward. Chicken shits like you are smart because you have to work out how to get out of things. How to phrase things well.' He closes his eyes. 'My wife ran off with a white bastard. A tea planter's son. Menaka was barely a year old.'

'That's disgusting. But they don't know that –'

'It almost killed me.' Uncle Thilak has a coughing fit, so I hold a hanky to his mouth. 'I wanted to kill that white bastard, but instead I found God and when I say God, I mean arrack. Arrack and valium and stress and strain and blind ambition – and I forgot about my kids.'

I bow my head. The old man is not confessing to anything new. Yet, it's breaking him and I think he's beginning to hate himself. 'It's understandable really, you know –'

'My wife came back,' he says. 'Less than a year later, she came back because she wanted to see her kids. But I stopped her.'

'They don't know this?' I ask.

'I wanted her to be punished,' he says. 'For cheating on me, with a bloody prick of a white man, so I destroyed her. Broke her down in court, tarnished her name, took every bit of dignity she had and crushed it. She was a selfish woman back then. Hot-headed, full of herself, so I didn't feel bad about what I did. But it was not her who suffered the most.'

'The kids?' I ask.

'Menaka mainly.' He pulls me down with surprising strength, almost smothering me. 'I let her believe her mother never wanted her. If she knew her mother had come back for her...if she knew... you must find a way to tell her.' He slaps my back. 'You find the bloody way to tell her...'

'That'll bring you peace?' I ask.

'If they serve peace in hell.' He nods. 'If they serve peace in hell. Bring my daughter in please.'

Menaka enters the room. Her eye make-up zig-zags down her face. Resting her head on her father's shoulder, she doesn't say anything. Just holds his hand.

He signals for me to hold his other hand.

'I was a bad father.' Uncle Thilak waits a moment or two, possibly hoping Menaka will contradict him. 'But I've been a good grandfather, no?'

'Surprisingly good,' Menaka says.

'The best,' I say.

'You two must do what's right for Kiki,' he says. 'That's all I ask of you.'

I drift off to sleep with my head on the corner of Uncle Thilak's bed, waking to Menaka's voice. 'He's not breathing,' she says. Calm. Dignified. She kisses his forehead three, four, five times.

Her head is on his thighs and she holds one of his hands in both of hers. 'Sorry, Thathi,' she says. 'Sorry.'

Sliding down off him, she collapses into a heap on the floor.

I know I must comfort her. Whatever has gone on between us, I know I have to look after her.

So I hug her and I feel like I am holding Kiki.

I know why I loved this woman. Why I always will. She gave me my baby girl.

'We must do the right thing,' she says.

twenty-nine

Uncle Thilak is being cremated thirty-six hours after he died. The crematorium is on the road that leads up to the golf club, which is fitting because that was his home away from home.

He had left instructions with his lawyer and will executioner, Priyanga, to ensure that there is no funeral. No fanfare. No state dignitaries and no granddaughters.

So it is me, in my white trousers and shirt. No doubt, if alive, Uncle Thilak would say I look naked. Aiya has arrived from Sydney and is dressed like me, and his so called sari-wearing wife is in a cream cotton dress. Menaka is in black, with a veil and hat. How she got this outfit together so quickly I don't know. Maybe she planned for it.

We are the only people here.

Uncle Thilak wanted his ashes to be scattered in the bunker of the fourteenth hole, because he said he spent so much time in there.

So with special permission from the club, either through love or fear that he will haunt them, they close the thirteenth, fourteenth and fifteenth holes for half an hour.

Uncle Thilak wanted Kiki here for this part of proceedings, so Caroline brings her. We each take turns scattering some ashes, and then we bow our heads.

It's midday, so the sun burns the back of my neck.

On the way home, Kiki is on my lap. Another excuse not to use the car seat.

'I'm sad,' she says.

'I am too, baby.'

'I miss him.'

I kiss her head. 'You promised him something...'

'He made me.'

'Can you tell me what?' I ask.

'It's a secret.' She zips her mouth shut. 'I will never tell.'

Caroline goes to bed straight after Kiki. I tell her I'm fine as I have been expecting and preparing for this loss for a while. I pour myself an arrack and look to my right, to Uncle Thilak's chair, and I want to tell him about Kiki's day. Like I always did.

For much of Kiki's life, I haven't had a wife to speak to about my daughter. So it was always Uncle Thilak.

If I talked to him about anything else, he told me to shut it. But if it was Kiki, his eyes lit up, even when the cancer had dressed them blank.

It hasn't hit me that he is dead. Maybe it never will. He was just a miserable old man who never seemed to like me.

But I miss him and, in some ways, I loved him. Maybe because he was the only person I had to share my love of Kiki with, and that's a hell of a bond.

In the last stages of his illness, when he couldn't drink or smoke, he still used to make me pour him a whisky or an arrack, and that is what I do tonight.

And I talk to him, like I used to do even when it was unclear whether or not he could hear or understand me.

For much of the last couple of months, he was just a body without a mind.

But seeing Kiki that last time gave him spark. We did the right thing by coming back.

I don't believe in heaven or hell, or the afterlife in any way at all. Yet, it's beginning to make sense to me now why people do. I wouldn't be talking to him if I didn't hope that he was somewhere, maybe just a soul, but somewhere.

I shake my head. Crazy talk. Still, I light a cigarette for him, and read him what I have written so far.

I remember about the drawer of things he left for Kiki and I know I have to check what's in it before Kiki does. It could be anything, really. Yet, I'm not surprised to find black-and-white silver-framed photographs of a lady who must be Menaka's mother, Uncle Thilak's wife, Kiki's grandmother. With it, Legbreaker Gunesekera's business card. If Kiki or Menaka ever want to find her, he's the man.

I will never know if Menaka intended to do the right thing or not. Uncle Thilak knew all along that there was no risk of her taking Kiki from me because he left no money to his granddaughter. He split his fortune three ways: half to Aiya and a quarter each to Menaka and me.

For whatever reasons, Menaka dropped her claims for custody of Kiki as long as she could see her once a week.

It's been eighteen weeks since we reached this settlement and she has seen Kiki eleven times, which I think isn't so bad.

Kiki calls her Ammi, and she calls Caroline Mama, so maybe in her mind she is lucky to have two mothers.

Even though Caroline and I are to be married in nine weeks, she still allows me half an hour on most nights to have a drink with Uncle Thilak. It was proving expensive to keep pouring the old man a drink without him being there, but I keep a glass and a chair for him, just in case he ever drops in.

I tell him all my news. That I'm getting married to the blondie.

I can hear him calling me a jackass. A loser, an imperialist bastard. I can hear him telling me how to bring up Kiki. I can hear him asking if I've told Menaka about her mother. The truth is I haven't, yet, because I don't want to tarnish her memory of her father so soon after his death.

⋘✥⋙

Today, when I pick Kiki up from school, she fakes a cough halfway home. 'Have you forgotten something, Daddy?'

'I picked you up, did the groceries.'

'About Mama?'

'No, what do you...' I remember. 'Her birthday tomorrow.'

'Cake, present, flowers,' Kiki says.

'Cake, present, flowers, of course,' I say. 'Do you want me to drop you home for your nap first?'

'No way, Daddy, you'll mess it up without me.'

We end up buying Caroline a super cake, a massive bunch of red roses and a pink bicycle, which Kiki chooses. Kiki's a Rupasinghe, and sticking with tradition, I have to be ordered around by one.

At home I tell Kiki she has to go to bed for her nap, but she insists on going to see Seeya first.

I follow her up to his room and squat outside the door.

'Hi Seeya.' Kiki puts a hand on his bed. 'Again today, Daddy needed my help. Lucky I'm such a big girl now. Don't worry. Like you made me promise, I'll always look after the bugger.'

acknowledgements

The reclusive genius, tennis fanatic and reluctant sex-symbol Kanishka Gupta, my agent, who found a few publishers willing to take on this book and who led me, ultimately, to Amish Raj Mulmi at Hachette India.

It was a joy working with Amish, my editor; kind, encouraging, talented and efficient. Thank you for showing such enthusiasm for this book.

I am indebted, most of all, to the beautiful Neelini Sarkar. As Kanishka's Publishing Consultant, she recognised that the rushed novella I sent in to Writer's Side had potential and pointed out exactly what I should do to make it better. Her vision is exceptional, her ideas always spot on. Without her I would never have been published.

Robin Hiney, the only friend I have the courage to show my work to. He is honest enough to give me suggestions, dishonest enough to pretend he likes what I write. As has always been the case, I run everything I do by him.

To Kenny, Priyanga and Hafsa for little bits of help here and there. Initially I was quite private about this book, perhaps through a lack of confidence in it, but to those friends I spoke to about it, thanks for feigning interest.

To all at Cornerstones for the encouragement and the guidance: Helen Byrant, Ayisha Malik, Kathryn Price, Brett Hardman and Sharon Zink.

My mother-in-law, Rohini, is unlikely to make it this far in the book as she is too busy telling people on the phone how busy she is, but I'm very grateful to her and my dashing father-in-law, Nimal, and stunning sister-in-law, Bianca, for their kindness.

To my brother and sister, Sonam and Tashi, and my nephew and niece, Jack and Anna, for their humour, and to my brother-in-law Charlie for his attempts at humour.

Thanks to my incredible mother for everything, not least being the only person likely to buy this book voluntarily. She is the most positive person in the world and her MBE last year was so richly deserved.

My late father Kesang, who died of cancer in 2000. As original a man as you could find; the inspiration for the funny aspects of Thilak's character (but not the racism). While not brushing my hair into a side-parting, or playing pranks on me, he was my biggest (and only) fan.

Samantha, my wife and best friend; thanks for making this the first novel you ever finished, even if you only read it when I was watching. To Tara Mae, part-time joker, full-time daughter. Whatever the reception is for this book (if there is one), I have you two beauties to come home to everyday.

My appreciation and apologies to Sri Lanka, my favourite country. My book is fiction, so I have taken some liberties with facts and made up events. Yet, the truth is Sri Lankans are the warmest people in the world, and quite possibly the funniest.